3 WEEK LOAN

Please check all items for damages
before leaving the Library.
Thereafter you will be held
responsible for all injuries
to items beyond reasonable wear.

The Book of Murdock

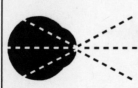

This Large Print Book carries the
Seal of Approval of N.A.V.H.

THE BOOK OF MURDOCK

MURDOCK

LOREN D. ESTLEMAN

THORNDIKE PRESS

A part of Gale, Cengage Learning

GALE
CENGAGE Learning

Detroit • New York • San Francisco • New Haven, Conn • Waterville, Maine • London

LARGE PRINT WESTERN EST

LIBRARY OF CONGRESS CATALOGING-IN-PUBLICATION DATA

Estleman, Loren D.
    The book of Murdock / by Loren D. Estleman. — Large print ed.
    353 p. cm. — (Thorndike Press large print western)
    "A Page Murdock novel."
    ISBN-13: 978-1-4104-2420-4
    ISBN-10: 1-4104-2420-0
    1. Murdock, Page (Fictitious character)—Fiction. 2. Outlaws—Fiction. 3. Texas—Fiction. 4. Western stories. gsafd 5. Large type books. I. Title.
    PS3555.S84B66 2010
    813'.54—dc22   2010008747

Published in 2010 by arrangement with Tom Doherty Associates, LLC.

Printed in the United States of America
1 2 3 4 5 6 7 14 13 12 11 10

To Lydia Morgan Hopper:
God bless the child

For there is not a just man upon earth, that doeth good, and sinneth not.

— ECCLESIASTES 7:20

THE SEVENTH ANGEL

And the seventh angel sounded . . . And the temple of God was opened in heaven, and there was seen in his temple the ark of his testament; and there were lightnings, and voices, and thunderings, and an earthquake, and great hail.
> — REVELATION 11:15–19

On the last day of my life I went into Chicago Joe's Coliseum and ordered a cognac. The place had another name now, but those of us who remembered when the town was put together with canvas and tobacco spit still called it Chicago Joe's, or just the Coliseum if a lady was listening. It was fitted out more like a private parlor than a saloon, with brocade curtains covering the passage to the separate room where ladies sent their serving girls to have their pails filled with beer, but once you knew the place you could never look upon mahogany and flocked paper again without getting thirsty. The cuspidors were lined with blue porcelain and there was a brass call box on the wall at the end of the bar where the staff kept track of orders from upstairs. None of its pointers had been moved off level; it was late morning, with floaters drifting in shafts of sunlight, and all the hostesses were asleep.

The bartender was a hairy-fisted relic of tin-pan days, a veteran of bare-knuckle fights in the camp. Scar tissue blistered his face and his milky right eye moved independently of its mate, like a cue ball rolling aimlessly on a billiard table at sea. "What's the occasion? Old Gideon's more your taste." He poured a swallow of French into a cordial glass and re-stopped the bottle right away; evaporation cost dear.

"Today's my birthday."

"Which one?"

"The latest."

"Many happy returns."

He didn't try to sound sincere and I didn't pretend he was. I'd arrested him once for selling cigars without a federal license and shot a generous customer over some official matter I'd forgotten. The man had lived but lost the use of an arm, and after that he'd counted his change more closely. There was no guild for stove-up ranch hands, and consequently no pension.

But despite past differences the bartender was in decent humor when I slung back the drink and ordered another. I fancied there was even a twinkle in his blind eye. For the world had come round: A mail robber I'd chased into a ravine, shattering his mare's cannon, had been released by congressional intervention and was in town looking for redress for the loss of a favorite horse. The common wisdom was he was the better marksman and his reflexes were superior, he being younger. For once the common wisdom was right. I'd have been better off if I'd deprived him of a brother or a friendly banker, losses more easily forgotten; but pipe dreams ran higher than cognac.

I took more time with the second drink, pooling it on my tongue and letting it glide down, scraped a fifty-cent piece across the bar, and pocketed every penny that came back.

"And no more than justice it is," I heard the bartender mutter as I pushed out through the doors.

It was a clear crisp day — a regular Montana Particular — a little flinty with the wind skidding off the snowcaps on the Divide, setting my face tingling, flushed as it was from the good liquor. It wasn't cold enough to cover my best suit of clothes with bearskin or even heavy twill. The sky hurt to look at.

It depressed me beyond language. I'd buried my father on just such a day, and as I leaned on the shovel all I could think of was the splendor he'd missed. How much better to go into the ground with the clouds as black as weeds and weeping.

But no day is a good day to die. The Indians were as wrong about that as they were about everything else.

The local loafers were all out enjoying the first stretch of pleasant weather since the sodden thaw, smoking, yarning, scratching at the lively activity in their longhandles, and admiring the golden-brown arc their spittle made as it cleared the hitching rails and splashed into the muddy street. I knew a few of them to talk to, but they all withdrew inside or down the boardwalk as I approached, as nonchalant as spooked antelope. What I had was worse than smallpox. I tightened my left arm against my ribs just to feel the solid lump of the Deane-Adams in my armpit.

A water wagon passed, spilling its inevitable leakage from staves inadequately treated with pitch. I waited for it to clear, then stepped off the boards to cross Bridge

Street. I'd just come out of the shade of the porch when the shock came.

I heard the crash and identified it even as I was falling. I hadn't counted on a carbine, or that it would be fired from a second-story window of the Bannack Hotel on the other side of Main. The echo growled in the mountains as I lay in the mud pedaling one leg for a purchase I couldn't find. A crowd gathered around. There's always a crowd to be had, no matter how empty the street at the start. You can't beat blood or free beer for civic interest.

I hoped they'd get the dates right on the stone. Hickok had made it only as far as thirty-nine, and mine is a competitive spirit.

■ ■ ■ ■ ■

I
JUDGE
BLACKTHORNE'S
EPISTLE TO THE
TEXICANS

■ ■ ■ ■ ■

ONE

"How much do you know about the Bible?"

"It's black, isn't it?"

Judge Harlan A. Blackthorne and I were seated in the library of the Helena Stockmen's Club on Fuller Street, drinking claret with a shard of rye, the Judge's own concoction, called Old Thunder's Gavel by the deputies who served him. The only book present was a hollowed-out copy of the *Montana Territorial Code* containing the pocket model Colt the Judge carried in response to the latest threat against his life. The club's reading material stood in presses in the dining room, clearing space for its much larger liquor supply inside oak cabinets in the room where we sat.

His expression betrayed a piety that didn't match his Satanic features and pitchfork beard. But as usual he shifted his annoyance to a less revealing subject. "Damn it, Deputy, I know your prejudice against displaying the badge of office, but you might pay me the respect of wearing it in my presence."

"Yes, Your Honor." I foraged it from a pocket and pinned it on. Blackthorne scowled whenever I addressed him by any title other than Judge. Anything else didn't quite fit my mouth, although I could get out a proper "sir" in times of admiration; and I did admire him, but I'd take a bullet through the star before I'd say it. He was a vain old rooster who never forgot an insult or a compliment.

He dismissed the shaft with a gesture that told me how deep I'd struck. I'd just returned from a messy errand in Oregon that had reflected badly on us both as well as on the federal court, and I hadn't scrupled to remind him I'd been against it from the start. That I was there at all when I should have been on leave while tempers cooled said he needed me for something unpleasant, and I was determined to let him twist until he got to the point.

"Do you seriously know nothing of Scripture?" he asked. "I'd expect someone of your frontier stock to have been brought up on sourdough and Jesus."

"Dugouts are designed for getting snowed in. There was always plenty of Jesus when the bread ran out. I caught a case of devotion, but it was like measles. You don't get it twice."

"Have you no faith apart from your oath to the Union?"

"I took it with my hand on a Bible. If I thought it was for more than show I'd have sworn on my pistol. I've seen good men die and bad men prosper, but never an angel to tip the scale. If I ever was going to, it would have been at Murfreesboro."

"Are you an atheist?"

"I never liked the ones who claimed to be. They all tried to convert me."

"An agnostic?"

"I don't know."

He frowned as if I'd made an inappropriate jest. The truth was I didn't know what the word meant. I learned later it was of recent coinage.

"But you can sham belief," he said.

I'd no idea where the conversation was headed, but already I didn't care for it by half. The Judge was a regular-attending Presbyterian; whether that was for community relations or because he thought as much of his immortal soul as he did of the bench wasn't something he shared with those of us who provided him with defendants, and I doubted he was any more forthcoming with his prosecutor or the local leaders he met with formally and at poker. I'd have suspected him of leading up to a dire announcement if I weren't certain he intended to live forever.

I said, "I can be an eagle or a duck. Which one depends on the job."

"I haven't said there is a job. You're on inactive duty."

"That's true. As long as we're just chewing the fat, where do you stand on Pharaoh's daughter finding baby Moses in the rushes? She spun a good yarn, but that was the last time anyone believed a story like it."

"That's blasphemous."

"You ought to know. You're using Holy Writ to recruit me for work."

"You're hopeless."

"If I didn't have hope I'd be dead in Oregon."

The forbidden subject jerked him back onto the rails. He rang for the steward, a bald, leathery Scot in a rusty tailcoat who'd navigated for Lewis and Clark and Noah, and asked him to fetch the big atlas from the dining room.

When he returned lugging a cloth-bound volume the size of a saddle blanket, Blackthorne opened it across the arms of his chair, made heretical marks on one of the watercolor maps with a gravity pen, and sat back. I rose and circled behind to study it over his shoulder. With a sinking heart I recognized the outline of Texas, my least favorite place after Dakota; which to be fair to Dakota had only been the place where I'd almost been slaughtered by the Cheyenne Nation. Even worse, the marks he'd made were in the panhandle, a spot that existed because the same incessant wind that blew it away daily blew in fresh dirt from Mexico. The panhandle would disappear when the sand ran out.

"I've marked the sites of five armed robberies that have taken place in the past six months," Blackthorne said. "Two banks, an Overland stage, two trains. The banks aren't our concern, but mail was stolen from the Overland and one of the trains, and that is."

"What's the matter with the federal court in Austin?"

"Its deputy marshals are spread thin over a jurisdiction the size of France. The Texas Rangers, who normally can be depended upon to fill the gap, are busy patrolling the border of Mexico for *bandidos*. Governor Ireland has asked us for our help, after Isaac Parker in Arkansas turned him down for obvious reasons."

Parker was the only U.S. jurist who was

more put-upon than Blackthorne, with seventy-four thousand square miles of Indian Territory to tame by way of two hundred deputy marshals and a gallows in Fort Smith the size of a frigate. The two despised each other for reasons unknown to me, but they were united in their contempt for interferers from Washington.

"Still, five robberies. We can scrape up that many in parts of Montana most seasons. What's our end?"

"Method of operations was nearly identical in all five. That suggests the same band. At the pace they're going, they'll fish out their current waters in short order and relocate. I'd rather we fought them on Texas ground than ours. Innocent bystanders there are spread out more and less likely to take a stray round."

That was thin even for him, but I didn't press the point. If he were going to confide the truth to me, he wouldn't have bothered to put up even so transparent a lie. In any case we were interrupted by the antique steward, who'd returned to ask if we wanted more refreshment. To my surprise the Judge nodded, and the Scot took from a cabinet a cut-glass decanter and from another a bottle of Monongahela and mixed their contents in our empty glasses. Blackthorne was a one-drink, one-cigar man by order of his physician, who had seen him through a heart attack, and no one who answered to the Judge had ever asked for seconds in his presence.

Except me, of course; but this was the first time he'd joined me in the rebellion.

If the steward noticed that a valuable book from the club's collection had been defaced, his expression didn't show it, and he left without remark. Membership was restricted to owners of ranches exclusively, but although Blackthorne held no title to a single square inch of real property, an exception had been made in his case because he'd tried and convicted rustlers with such Old Testament fervor that not so much as a stolen pair of horns had crossed the territorial line in more than a year. It stood to reason that until one did, he could scribble dirty pictures all over the walls of the reception room on Ladies' Night without a mark appearing against his name in the register.

He closed the atlas and slid it over the arm of his chair until it leaned against the side. For a few moments I watched him shifting his weight on the cushions in search of a compromise between his bony angles and the arrangement of horse hair in the upholstery. The only seat that really suited him was the one behind the high bench in the courthouse. Just because he was physically restless, however, didn't mean he wasn't complacent in his mind. He knew I would raise the subject sooner or later.

I took a long draught of the Gavel and gave him his way. "The Bible."

"I take solace from it often. The beauty of the Song of Solomon stands out against its background of war, plague, and human sacrifice. I was reminded of it when 'Whispering Hope' swept through town last year; I was trying a case of rape, murder, and dismemberment, and the strains came through the window as an eyewitness was testifying. I was comforted by the reflection that ugliness and beauty — hell and redemption, if you will — have abided side by side on earth since the beginning. All the changes are superficial. I wonder if the Israelites gathered in the courtyard of the palace to predict Judgment Day the way our street philosophers do on Catholic Hill?"

"If so, and Solomon's father David was in charge, he'd have stuck them in the front lines and given them the first look."

"So some of the Word remained with you after all."

"Not enough to get me from the Kingdom of Israel to the panhandle of Texas."

He ran a finger around the top of his glass, drawing a dull hum from the crystal. He made some kind of decision and set it on his chairside table untouched. "Each of those robberies took place within three days' ride of Owen, a former buffalo-hunting center more lately concerned with sheepherding, with all the complications that represents with the local cattle interests. Full-time brigand is passing out of fashion. Increased numbers of law enforcement officers and the Pinkertons' stranglehold has forced many road agents into the cover of legitimate employment. Jesse James and the Youngers scorned the life of the working ranch hand, but most of the later breed has come out of line shacks and the bunkhouse and fly back into them between raids. My theory is you're more likely to find these highwaymen rounding up strays in Palo Duro Canyon than hiding out in some cave planning their next outrage.

"The challenge, of course, is to penetrate that close society without raising the alarm — sending them into flight or open confrontation with their loyal friends at their side. A band of officers would bring about the former, and a single man poking about would almost certainly end up bleaching his bones somewhere on the Staked Plain.

However, there is one profession that thrives on a healthy knowledge of the lives of the members of his community without arousing suspicion, and without prowling beyond his station and the various tables where he is invited to break bread."

I saw where he was heading then, and felt a nasty grin splitting my face. "I can stand for a cowhand because I've been one, and they took me for a saloonkeeper down in New Mexico because I know my way around a bar, but the first time I thump a pulpit, they'll smell brimstone clear to Chicago."

"You fail to appreciate the proposition. Men confide in their barbers, women in their dressmakers, but both sexes trust their ministers. In addition, the many social affairs that surround the church place the pastor in the best possible position to monitor gossip. No one knows his community better than the man who serves its spiritual needs."

"Get Ter Horst. His wife teaches Sunday school, and that sheep face of his belongs at the Last Supper."

"I considered him first, but he thought the plan profane. He threatened to resign."

"Whereas my soul's up for grabs. The star draws fire like a bottle on a fence rail, but I put it on when you ask. I won't reverse my collar for you. I never met a man struck by lightning who was decent company after we got past the obvious."

He smiled then, close-lipped without the teeth he wore only in the courtroom. "I felt certain once I scratched that infidel's hide I'd find a believer. You're too hard on yourself, Page. You have an ecclesiastical mien when you discuss a subject that arouses your passion. The rest is costuming."

That was when I knew I was beaten, although I argued my case a few more minutes just to make the conversation as disagreeable for him as it was for me. When Judge Blackthorne addressed me by my given name, there was no slack left in the leash.

Two

I asked how long I'd be in seminary. He said I was leaving for Texas in two weeks.

I stared. "That's barely time to get through Genesis."

"Once again you undervalue your abilities, and you know I regard false modesty a mortal sin. I've seen you plow through a thick field report without pausing to lick your thumb. Genesis is only sixty-six pages in the standard King James edition, and the whole thing's shorter than *Ben-Hur* by two hundred sixty. But then Lew Wallace always was prone to wander."

"How did you know that?"

"Every schoolboy knows he got lost on the way to Shiloh, leading to huge Union losses. It was a great victory for the army when he turned toward literature."

"I mean how did you know the number of pages in King James? I've met men who can recite it front to back who couldn't tell you that."

"As can I. As can a magpie, with as much comprehension of the spirit behind the words. Annex to that in my case a talent for figures." He tugged out his fine platinum watch, engraved with his name by President Polk for distinguished service during the war with Mexico; I assume a medal had come with it, but the watch and the bullet-chewed tricolor flag that hung on the wall of his chambers were the only souvenirs he displayed from that episode. "I know, for example, that of this moment you have eleven thousand, three hundred and forty-four minutes to make yourself intimate with the Book of Books before your train leaves. I caution you to use them all. There are Texans who can barely write their names but who will drag you through cactus if you overlook a comma in Ezekiel; again, a feat of exhibition rather than of faith. That panhandle country is undiverting and made to order for scholarly study."

"There's more to being a minister than reading and regurgitating verses. You haven't even told me my denomination."

"The vacancy you're filling was left by a Unitarian, which is the nearest thing established doctrine offers to religion à la carte.

We'll go one step further from popery and make you an evangelist. That way there will be no truck with arcane ceremony and personal strictures. You're free to take strong drink and fornicate, although I advise more than usual discretion in both pursuits. You're aware of *el ley del fugo*?"

"*La ley de la fuga.* The law of flight applies only to fleeing suspects. It's a license to slaughter."

"I sense error in both constructions, but I keep forgetting your season in New Mexico. It's been many years since I laid siege to Montezuma." The ends of his moustache turned down steeply. He hated to be caught in a mistake in the midst of a dissertation, and had found more than one attorney in contempt for correcting him in court. "The interpretation of the law becomes broader the farther one travels west or south of the more populous settlements. Your discovery alighting from the back porch of a married rancher upon his return home would not overstretch its spirit. Letter is another matter, but by the time a judgment was reached it would be unlikely to do you any material good."

"I can be killed for that here, and spend my last night in my own bed."

"Not yours, to be technical, but the point

is moot in any case, since you're making the journey. Texas is the only state that retains the privilege of secession, and some of the natives behave as if it's exercised it already. They're savages in silk hats."

"I know Texas, or most of it. That's why I came back to Montana."

"Riding herd, no doubt, upon its indigenous unchewable bovines." He tapped the arm of his chair with the edge of the watch as if it were his gavel. "A pulpit is not a saddle. You'll require a tutor for the public parts, as well as in the niceties of the rectory and parlor."

"I'm fresh out of suggestions. I don't know any of the ministers in town, and I'm not sure they'd take kindly to a stranger asking them how to defraud a flock of the faithful."

"I know an Episcopalian who'd shoot you as like as not with the pistol he uses to protect the sacramental wine. But I'd not send you out cold even in Helena on so delicate a mission. You'll want Eldred Griffin; *Father* Griffin, though I'd sound him out before I employed the title. I'm not certain if the custom of addressing ex officios as 'President' and 'Governor' extends to the clergy, and this fellow may take it amiss whatever the protocol." He rang for the steward and asked for envelopes and writing paper. The man withdrew, taking with him the big atlas, which he'd retrieved without asking — a veiled reference, I thought, to the Judge's desecration of its contents.

"A Catholic priest?" I asked.

"Defrocked. Distasteful term. One pictures a bishop tearing off the man's vestments in the churchyard and stomping his chalice flat."

"I hope he's not a colorful old character. I draw them like flies."

"You'll have no difficulty on that account. He's not many years older than you, and according to the Reverend Clay of the Presbyterian church, he suffers from chronic melancholia. Mr. Webster defines black as the absence of color."

The steward returned with a sheaf of foolscap and some envelopes. Blackthorne took two of each, sent him away with the rest, and shook ink into the business end of his pen. Using the table at his elbow, he spent some minutes writing, signed both pages in his elaborate hand, waved them dry, folded them into envelopes, and addressed each. He tucked in the flaps and held them out.

"The first will introduce you to Griffin.

Don't lose the second; it's for the captain of the Texas Rangers in Wichita Falls, who will prepare you for what to expect in Owen. I know I can trust you not to steal a look at them."

I opened each of the envelopes in turn and read the letters while he seethed. They were headed by the name of the Helena Stockmen's Association in halftone letters and a steel-point engraving of the club's brick headquarters. I refolded them and put them back, tapping the Texas-bound envelope with a finger. "Judge Blackthorne's Epistle to the Texicans?"

"You try my patience, Deputy. Did you think they contained instructions to assassinate you?"

"Anytime someone says he can trust me it means I can't trust him. What are the odds the thought never crossed your mind?"

"It's crossing it now."

"Am I really one of the most reliable officers in the federal system?"

"That depends on the area in which one relies upon you. Captain Jordan has slain sixteen men in the line of duty, whereas I'm told former Father Griffin is drawn to straight talk with no embroidery. For those reasons you may get along with both. Then again, you may not for the very same reasons. I still receive letters from the White House in response to calls for your extradition to Canada on behalf of the North West Mounted Police."

"It doesn't sound like this Captain Jordan wastes much time writing letters." I slid the envelopes into my inside breast pocket next to the underarm rig I wore in town.

"Were I you, I would cosset him at every opportunity. The Rangers are known for recruiting their officers on the basis of results rather than strict conformity to the rule of law."

"Cosset Jordan, talk turkey with Griffin. So long as I don't mix them up I can't go wrong."

Blackthorne smiled. I preferred it when he wore his teeth. I asked where I could find Griffin.

"In the Catholic cemetery."

Every time I returned to Helena, it seemed, more brick buildings had been erected to replace frame structures built on the same sites. This was because the city burned down every few years, and fireproofing is more effective than reeducating residents in the proper use of flame. One day the whole place would be brick, like Chicago, and it would be time for me to move on, because there's no room in civilization for a fellow with bark left on him.

The Cathedral of the Sacred Hearts of Jesus and Mary was one of the oldest local landmarks constructed of that sturdy material, and had sheltered many refugees from blazes under its spiky-crowned bell tower. I climbed Catholic Hill and discovered something new since I was there last: a large structure — brick, of course — risen in place of the wooden boarding school of Saint Vincent's Academy, where the nuns of the order taught children their letters as well as Numbers. It had burned or been torn down and replaced. But Sacred Hearts still dominated the hill.

I swore they'd done the work during my brief visit to Oregon, but then a lot more time had passed since I'd been near that church or any other. I didn't even know for sure what faith I'd fallen out of; my father never told me just Who he prayed to when he set his trap line in Blackfoot country, and my mother had kept her old gods to herself. I would be a challenge to instruct. My knuckles hurt just thinking about it.

Farther down the street, inside a grille fence topped with iron fleurs-de-lis, slumber the Catholic settlers of Last Chance Gulch, along with others of the same persuasion, under crosses and tablets and the odd bugling angel. But cemetery populations are continually expanding without attrition, and a larger lot had been purchased on the edge of town to accommodate later arrivals and marble vaults for the well-heeled.

Even old graves need tending, however, and vandals and thieves with spades need to be discouraged. A dwelling had been built for caretakers and their families on the last plot of unturned earth — some said atop the bones of forgotten pioneers whose wooden markers had burned or been carried away. It was a doll's house really, designed along the lines of the stately mansions of the suddenly rich on Benton Avenue and Lawrence Street, but scaled down to proportions more appropriate to its humble tenants. It was the same mansard roof, the same mullioned panes in Roman arches, the same gracious wraparound porch; but twelve paces would take you from the front door into the backyard, and even from the outside you could tell that a man not much taller than myself would have to duck when he climbed the stairs to the second story. And I am not tall.

I worked the bell pull and took off my hat when the door opened, as I would have upon entering a place of worship. The man who opened it was in his middle forties, my height (I wondered if he'd been hired for his slight stature, to preserve the plaster ceilings), and to my observation the owner of the only other shaven male chin and upper lip west of Pennsylvania. His cheeks were high ovals, his hair cut short and black without gray, and his eyes were that pale shade of blue that photographers have to touch up on the glass plate to keep them from reproducing dead white. He wore neither coat nor collar, but with his black waistcoat buttoned and white shirt fastened to the throat he appeared fitted out to preach the gospel in any church I'd ever entered.

"Father Griffin?"

"Eldred Griffin." He had a low, even voice that never strayed above or below a straight line — or so I thought then. It had the quality of a chant. "You're Page Murdock." He touched a pocket in his waistcoat. I'd sent him Judge Blackthorne's letter by way of a messenger, with a note of my own, but I hadn't expected him to keep either on his person. The way he touched it made me think of an amulet to ward off — well, me.

I showed him the simple six-pointed star. "Am I interrupting anything?"

"Only my retirement."

I pocketed the star and took out his response. "You invited me here."

He glanced at it without interest. "It isn't my hand."

"Eldred, you know very well it's mine." This was a new voice.

He half turned from the doorway, giving me a straight shot across the shallow entryway at a small woman standing framed in an arch leading to the rest of the house. Her hair, brown with streamers of gray, was skinned back and fastened behind her head, and her face was round, without a single feature that called attention to itself. She wore a dark brown dress, nearly black, and plain to the point of pride; a placket concealed the buttons. An egg-shaped stone the color of slate in an old-fashioned setting showed on the index finger of her right hand, folded over its mate at her waist. It was her only ornament.

Griffin didn't forget his manners. "My wife, Esther. Page Murdock."

My hat was already off, so all I could do was incline my head. I had the impression she was older than her husband. Her gaze acknowledged my gesture, then went to him. "How often have you said you wanted to pass on what you know?" she asked. "I thought it an opportunity to learn whether you have the gift."

"You might have discussed it with me before you acted."

"Oh, Eldred. When have you ever discussed anything with anyone? If I hadn't acted, you would still be clipping weeds ten years from now."

"It's honest labor."

"Not if it's not what God intended."

"He speaks to you, whereas with me He is silent."

"Mr. Murdock did not come here to listen to us quarrel. Invite him in."

"You know what he wants. To pose as a man of the cloth in order to catch a rogue. Sin for sin, and I am to be his accomplice. 'Speak not in the ears of a fool: for he will despise the wisdom of thy words.' "

" 'The integrity of the upright shall guide them,' " she said.

" '. . . but the perverseness of transgressors shall destroy them.' "

"Should I be taking notes?" I asked.

THREE

"In which faith were you raised?" Griffin asked.

"Christianity," I said. "I'm pretty sure."

"I meant which church."

"I was born six thousand feet up in the Bitterroots. I never saw a church until I was almost grown."

His pale eyes clouded. "Your parents were savages?"

"Only my father. My mother was some part Indian."

"Which tribe?"

"Nez Perce, I think."

"You don't know?"

"I wasn't encouraged to ask questions."

"And so with those qualifications you chose to enter law enforcement."

"No one chooses that. I just sort of drifted into it after the buffalo ran out. In between I punched cows and shot wolves in the winter for the bounty, but I made too thorough a job of it. When wolves got scarce I became a drunk for a while and got to know a few jails. In one of them the sheriff turned out to be an old bunkmate. He told me the U.S. marshal was hiring here in Helena. It was the only work I could get where my recent history didn't count against me."

"And how long have you been about it?"

"Ten years last April. Felons don't seem to run dry like buffalo and wolves and whiskey."

"A fortunate turn for the citizenry. Road agentry is the only calling you haven't answered."

"I disagree. The frontier keeps changing. There's always a paying position that didn't exist last week. What did you do before you became a priest?"

"I was an altar boy."

We were seated in a pair of split-bottom chairs in a room he called his study, a dim cell at the top of a flight of stairs you practically had to crawl up on hands and knees to keep from cracking your skull on the square timber across the top. One wall slanted with the roof and the rest were a jumble of books stuck in at every angle between two-inch-thick pine shelves. More books and loose papers climbed corners to the low papered ceiling. A lamp with a blackened chimney smoked on a small writing table near his chair, stinging my eyes while illuminating little but itself. The room smelled of coal oil and moldy bindings.

One queer thing I'd noticed: None of the rooms I'd passed through on the way there contained a visible religious symbol of any kind. The study was no exception. I'd never been in a Catholic household that didn't display a large crucifix or a picture of Jesus somewhere prominent.

He returned to my origins. He would be one of those biblical scholars who cut Methusaleh in half to count the rings. "The Nez Perce are an intelligent people. Large cranial capacity. I taught them at the Saint Ignatius Mission when I was in seminary. You favor them in the jaw. In the forehead, not so much."

"My father came from Aberdeen. He used to smash stoneware jugs with his head to win bets."

"You must have been proud."

"Grateful for the inheritance. I've stopped more than my share of pistol butts and I can still walk a straight line."

"You and I are not of the same flesh," he said. "I cannot think of any other circumstances that would place us both in one

42

room." He leaned forward as if to rise. "I'm not going to help you. The only reason I didn't turn you away at the door is I'd never be quit of it as long as Esther is around to remind me."

As if in response to her name, his wife knocked and entered, carrying a brass lamp and a silver tea set on a tray. She was the only one of us who didn't have to lower her head to clear the doorway. She set the tray on a squat square footstool stacked with volumes — there wasn't a bare horizontal space in the room, but this one at least was level — traded lamps, and blew out the one that had been fouling the air. The room brightened immediately. I don't know that it had entirely to do with a clear chimney and a well-trimmed wick.

She poured for us both. I don't like tea, but when she'd mentioned brewing it I'd assented, because I wanted her present for what I did then. I fished a leather poke from my side pocket and placed it on the tray where the pot had stood. It clanked.

"I'm authorized by the United States District Court for the Territory of Montana to offer you a hundred dollars in gold for divinity lessons," I said. "Judge Blackthorne advised me to pay half in advance and the rest upon completion. I'm putting it all on the table. The risk of flight in your case seems small."

"It used to be thirty pieces of silver. The treasury must be in good condition."

"Eldred, the man is our guest."

I said, "It's more than twice what I earn in a month, but we're asking for a season's instruction in two weeks. The object of betrayal is a gang of highwaymen, not Jesus."

"You're overlooking the rest of the congregation, who will come to you in search of guidance. 'Have ye not spoken a lying divination —' " He broke off with a sidelong glance at his wife. It occurred to me that her knowledge of the Bible ran deeper than his. I seemed to have stumbled into an old argument.

"It won't be a lie if you teach him the proper words."

"A profane man profanes holy words merely by speaking them."

"The sword of God is not so brittle," she said. "And Mr. Matthews has refused to extend us any more credit at the meat market."

I'd gambled right. It was the men who were winning the West, but it was the women who kept the books.

Griffin sat back a fraction of an inch, fixing me with his pale eyes. "Were you baptized?"

"I've been up to my chin in the Canadian and all the way under in the Yellowstone. I almost drowned that time."

He looked at Esther. "Are you not yet convinced whom he represents? Must he sprout horns and hooves?"

"The Prince of Lies is not so clumsy or we would not fear him." She turned to me with the teapot in one hand and a full cup and saucer in the other. "Have you really never been christened in the faith?"

I shook my head.

"There's the end of it," Griffin said. "Tell Matthews I'll eat potatoes and miss Purgatory."

"Don't be theatrical. You hate potatoes. The solution is simple. Mr. Murdock will submit to be baptized, and we shall ask him to join us at supper tomorrow night after his lesson. Pork chops, I think." She handed me the cup and saucer, gave the other to her husband, and set down the pot, scooping the sack of coins from its path and putting it in the pocket of her plain apron, all in the same movement. Then she lifted the tray and left.

For a moment the only sound in the room was me blowing on my tea. I looked across at him. "I don't suppose you'd care to do the honors."

"It wouldn't be sanctified. I'm no longer a priest."

"I'll ask Reverend Clay, then."

The crease between his brows deepened. It had looked like a scar to begin with. "The Presbyterian?"

"I'm posing as an evangelist. How good does it have to be?"

"Mother of God." He crossed himself. "Is there a sacred thing you don't hold in scorn?"

"I like the idea of the Good Samaritan. As for the rest, no one died for my sins. I wasn't born yet."

"By which I take you to mean you've invented some of your own."

"I'd be guilty of vanity if I said I had. I confess I've broken a Commandment or two in order to keep others."

"Do not use the word *confess* in my presence. The common belief is priests are unworldly and therefore unschooled in the wickedness of man. Those who subscribe to the theory have never sat in the darkness listening to a parishioner gloat over the details of unspeakable evil under the pretense of absolution. Nearing the end I became convinced that no number of Hail

Marys would spare them the pit. Meanwhile I retired to the rectory each evening bearing their burden as well as my own."

"Is that why you left the priesthood?"

He sipped tea, drawing it in with a sucking noise like a horse drinking water, and set his cup in its saucer with a click. It seemed to place a full stop to the conversation. "No doubt you think that having chosen evangelism you've avoided the intolerable yoke of dogmatic principle. What the informed laity lacks in formal training it more than makes up for in passion. Have you ever attended a tent meeting?"

"No."

"There is always one about, every Sunday in mild weather. You and I will attend the next. What do you intend to wear on this southwestern sojourn?"

I ran a thumb under the left lapel of my coat. He shook his head slowly. I said, "Not black enough?"

"Not humble enough. A made-to-order suit on a minister's back means a hand in the collection plate."

"I can't find a fit in a ready-made that has room for this." I spread the coat to show him the Deane-Adams in its suspender scabbard.

The skin of his face drew taut. "A righteous man arms himself with righteousness only."

"I consulted Samson and David on the matter. They came to a different conclusion."

"Do not seek to banter with me in Holy Writ. I will bury you, and we haven't time for it. You must not carry a pistol into a house of God."

"The last time I was in one I didn't see a gun check at the door. I'm going to Texas to break up a gang. If I save a soul, it's in the line of a collateral benefit. I've heard stories of pocket Bibles stopping bullets, but I don't credit them. Bandits carry heavy calibers as a rule."

He started to drink again, but his hand shook. He set cup and saucer on the writing table. "At least promise me you won't brandish it in church."

"I could, but it'd be a lie. They build churches and saloons from the same green wood and there are men who'd as soon bust a cap in a convent as in a brothel. I won't make a point of the business without good cause, I can swear to that much. That's why I need a coat that won't show a bulge."

"Pick one off the shelf a size too large. No, two sizes; the more shapeless the better. Bundle it in your bedroll, and when you reach your destination don't be too conscientious about brushing and pressing. You can't preach convincingly about a camel passing through the eye of a needle if you look as if you'd get stuck yourself."

"Should I let out my whiskers and chew a plug?"

"Assuredly not. You must be clean in your habits and appearance. Does it not sting your professional pride when you encounter a slovenly peace officer?"

"I've trusted my life to a few. But I understand. A bad lawman paints us all. I'll pack a razor and look to my nails."

"Clean them, don't pare them. And under no circumstances allow a barber to shave you. Fifteen cents for a haircut is as much as most ministers can afford, and they will forego a meal to avoid becoming shaggy. Fortunately, sustenance will not be a problem. Most parishioners consider having even a mediocre minister to their homes for dinner the same as purchasing an indulgence." He touched his flat belly. "Mind you, don't be taken in by the conventional belief that all country wives are superb cooks. You'd be wise to carry a sack of peppermints in your pocket to settle your stomach."

"I didn't realize the work was so danger-ous."

Nothing like a smile crossed his features. "Many men — out here in particular — make the mistake of confusing a cassock with a skirt. They have no concept of the level of courage required to walk the path of the lamb in a den of lions. Any fool can muster the strength to face a mortal enemy. Only one man in a thousand can find it within him to turn his back on one. Are you that man?"

I hesitated for the first time in the dis-course. "I don't know."

"An honest answer at last. Have you a Bible?"

"I own one. I didn't bring it. It seemed like carrying firewood to the forest."

"Bring it with you next time. It will save passing the text back and forth." He turned in his chair and lifted a volume the size of a traveling desk off the pile of books on his writing table — one-handed; his hands were slim and white, but as strong as a harvester's — opened it in his lap, and hooked on a pair of wire-rimmed spectacles from a waistcoat pocket.

And so began the catechism.

FOUR

I returned to my furnished room past midnight, limp as a bar rag. A hundred voices were shouting Bible passages in my head. Sunday school with Eldred Griffin was like digging postholes all day in the desert, and I'd done that too.

By gray dawn I was back in his study. He looked as fresh as I felt stale, wearing a clean collarless shirt with his waistcoat and trousers brushed and creased in the right places (he had no one to impress with his poverty) and a shine on his elastic-sided boots, round-heeled though they were.

That day began as did the next four, with the same question:

"Are you baptized yet?"

My answers varied:

"Not in the last six hours."

"I haven't had the chance."

"Reverend Clay went shooting."

"I'm catching a cold."

"I forgot."

On each occasion he made no comment, snapping open his leviathan Bible and directing me to turn to the passage before him in mine. He'd marked his place with a piece of razor strop scraped thin as flannel. My copy was bound in supple leather for traveling, with all the gold leaf worn off the outside lettering and its dog-eared pages rubbed nearly transparent at the edges, like a marked deck of cards. It had been left to me by Dad Miller, a deputy marshal who'd taught me two-thirds of what I knew about the hunting of men, including a posthumous lesson: Place the same faith in your friends as you do in your enemies. He'd had his throat cut while on watch by a member of his own posse.

Each day we interrupted our labors for breakfast, noon dinner, and supper. Esther Griffin was a good simple cook who skimped a bit on salt and pepper, but kept vinegar in a cruet on the table for my use; neither she nor her husband touched it. We ate meat on two evenings and crackles every morning, so I concluded that she had made peace with the butcher. We spread lard on slabs of coarse bread and washed everything down with chicory coffee and water, which she drew from a well uphill of the cemetery.

She baked bread twice that first week and on Saturday a peach pie made from preserves sent to her by a sister in Michigan whom she hadn't seen in seven years. I gathered that although she belonged to a large family, this sister was the only member who stayed in touch. I assumed the break had something to do with Griffin's having quit the priesthood, but later I learned I was wrong. Anyway the pie was good, if the crust was a little doughy; she blamed the woodstove, which listed toward the corner where a stack of bricks had been inserted in place of a broken leg.

Conversation at table centered around food, and if it weren't for the preserves. I'd never have found out about the sister and Esther's estrangement from the rest of her people. Griffin never failed to thank her for cooking, and he always pronounced the grace. "Never defer this duty to anyone else when you're a guest," he told me the first time I joined them. "Your hosts will be too polite to refuse, but they'll resent you for it. The reason for having you over is to gain a place at God's table, and if you don't put in a good word, their chances are no better than even."

"Is there anything else I should know?"

"Eat with your fingers if they eat with

theirs, but if they're too self-conscious to pick up a chicken leg in your presence, use a knife and fork. Don't let anyone see you pluck stray hairs from your food. And come prepared with plenty of fresh gossip."

"Isn't that violating some kind of oath?"

"The seal of the confessional doesn't extend to what you overhear in ordinary discourse, and doesn't exist at all outside the Roman Catholic Church. You must sing for your supper, especially if you want to hear what else is taking place among the congregation. The more garrulous the minister, the less laconic the host. That is the reason for this charade, is it not?"

"Still, it steers pretty close to bearing false witness."

He frowned at the bit of potato on his fork. It was the only vegetable I ever saw him eat, and he seldom did so without showing distaste. If it weren't for that I think he'd have come down with scurvy long before. "That raises another point. Never sermonize beneath another man's roof. He works six days a week only to be told on Sunday morning he is going to hell. He won't tolerate it in the afternoon."

"More cabbage?" Esther offered me the bowl.

I gained weight during that period, something I rarely did. Gluttony has never been one of my sins. I was used to bolting a steak in a saloon or a bowl of rabbit stew at a stage stop in order to keep from fainting and falling out of the saddle; sweets and savory seldom slowed me down when there was light out and miles to make. However, the ordeal upstairs made me ravenous. I think Esther Griffin enjoyed serving something other than bread and meat to someone other than herself, and took special care in the preparation. When she brought out the pie, she surprised Griffin by pouring a glass of cold milk for me from an earthenware pitcher.

"I traded Mrs. Nordström three eggs for a quart from her Maybelle," she said. She kept chickens in a little pen out back.

Griffin asked how she'd kept it cold.

"In the well, where else? You won't have an icebox in the house."

"Certainly not, with the market only three hundred yards away. The amount those pirates in the ice house demand for water and cold, God's own bounty, will revisit them at end of days." He was as pinchpenny as any country preacher.

"It's very good." I have a weakness for cold milk.

Griffin said, "I suppose this means no eggs

with our fatback tomorrow morning."

"It means hotcakes. I saved two."

His mood lightened then, and he spent several minutes in praise of Esther's hotcakes.

"Don't bore the man, Eldred. He'll find out tomorrow whether they taste like sunshine or black midnight."

He stopped talking and resumed eating. He touched on human whenever his wife was in the room. The rest of the time he was a slot machine that paid out in Scripture.

The sixth day of my training was Sunday. I came expecting a short lesson, as surely Griffin still attended morning services, and when he opened the door wearing a coat and hat I began to hope for a holiday. The coat was rusty and appropriately rumpled, and stove blacking had been applied to the kettle-shaped crown of his hat where the nap had worn off. He had on a stiff gutta-percha collar and a green cravat. When he asked about baptism, that's when I told him I'd forgotten.

"Come with me." He bustled me out the door and drew it shut behind him.

"Where are we going?"

"Where every nonheathen goes on Sunday."

"What about Mrs. Griffin?"

"She never attends church."

That surprised me more than when he'd told me there was no mention of apples in Genesis. I didn't even think to ask if it meant he'd married a heathen.

He'd hired a buggy and a shaggy gray. He left the whip in its socket and steered with the lines and short whistles. I'd suspected he avoided Sacred Hearts for reasons of his past, but when we left behind two Protestant churches, I got curious. Genuine wonder set in when we crossed the city limits and took the road that led to the Rockies.

In the foothills, where frost tipped the blades of grass like candle wax, we topped a low swelling rise — Griffin using the whip now to keep us from bogging down in mud from the spring runoff — and came within sight of a large gray tent pitched at the top of the next, looking like the off spring of the massive peak rising beyond it from a tarn of ground fog into streamers of cloud. A hundred yards away from the tent, the nearest stretch of level earth held a dense assemblage of carriages, buggies, and buckboards, and saddle horses browsing in the winterkill for tough new green shoots; it hardly seemed as if any form of transportation had been left in Helena, nor a dry hem or pair of boots among the men, women, and children who had picked their way up the hill. I heard a virile voice raised in song:

There's a place above all others,
where my spirit loves to be.
'Tis within the sacred shadow
of the cross of Calvary.

It was as clear as newly minted silver but rang like iron on iron. From that day to this I've never heard one to approach it for depth or distance. I felt it in the soles of my feet, and they were eighteen inches above the ground. Then the chorus came in:

In the shadow of the cross,
in the shadow of the cross;
there my spirit loves to be.
In the shadow of the cross.

These voices were an inexact mix of male and female, full-throated and tentative, on key and off by a country mile; not all of them finished at the same time, and there was one bray in particular that shrank my gums from my teeth at the top of the scale. There's always one, and he never misses a service. But the best of them was a torn hinge compared to the soloist:

> On the cross my Savior suffered,
> that He might atone for me.
> And I love the blessed shadow
> of the cross of Calvary.

I asked Griffin who it was.

"Lawrence Lazarus Little; I have doubts about the second name. That's his outfit." He inclined his head toward a sheeted Studebaker wagon standing near the entrance to the tent, with DR. L. L. LITTLE'S TRAVELING TABERNACLE painted in Barnum letters on the canvas. A pair of Percherons stood hitched to it, eighteen hands high unshod, switching braided tails at flies buzzing around their great round haunches. "He styles himself a doctor of divinity. I can't contest it, but whatever his credentials, when he lifts his voice to God, our heavenly father must either listen or strike up the celestial choir to drown it out."

"Where do you know him from?"

"Denver. Cheyenne. Omaha. Wherever the church sent me, there he was. For years I thought he was an imp sent to bedevil me, but I knew nothing then of the tent-show circuit. I doubt he's overlooked a major population center or a tin-pan mining camp since he answered the Call. If he were Catholic he'd be a cardinal by now."

"What church is he with?"

"Southern Baptist."

That was the last answer I wanted, because I'd already suspected the worst, and the presence in a dale fifty feet beyond the tent of an acre of standing water did nothing to cheer me. It was an old buffalo wallow, from its size as ancient as the veins of gold that remained in the mountains, and worn into a perfect bowl by a thousand dead shaggies. Jagged panes of ice ringed the edge like painted glass.

I waited until we'd found a place among the other horses and vehicles and stepped down. "If you think I'm going in that frozen puddle," I said, "you've had too much traffic with miracles. I'll take my chances with the lake of fire."

He let the lines drop to the ground. It was a livery animal and wouldn't wander away from others of its kind. "It's just water. Don't tell me you've never crossed a river in colder weather than this."

"Then I had something worth getting to on the other side."

"Not like what's waiting for you this time."

"Just because you taught me to recite a

few columns of verse doesn't mean you made me a believer."

He turned toward me. The shadow of his hat brim drew a mask around his washed-out blue eyes without concealing them; they seemed to glow like phosphor, but that's an old mesmerist's trick, and most spiritual counselors are students of the art. "Man is conceived in sin, and piles transgression upon transgression all the days of his life. The earth is nine parts water. Nine times nine would not begin to pale the stain of the first; not that brackish pond, and certainly not the paltry few drops the priests of my church sprinkle in a man's face, as if it came sixty dollars the barrel, and declare him cleansed. The Blood of the Lamb is a rare vintage and cannot be bought with Latin. The ceremony is a charming fraud, like confession, and like confession it fools none but fools. But it is the beginning of hope."

"Hope of what, salvation?"

"That's faith. Faith requires a higher power. Hope is the belief that you can reverse the course of your own descent. It's the only mortal thing the devil fears, or he would not banish it at his gate. It involves free will, which will always be the enemy of him who would throw bad after bad. I will turn a faithless man out into the world to carry the Word, I am that corrupt, but I will spend eternity in limbo before I turn out a creature without hope to poison the hearts of my brothers."

"So religion is free will. I thought it was the opposite."

"You thought nothing until God placed you in my charge."

"Judge Blackthorne said I was hopeless. I said he was wrong."

"Prove it."

I looked from him to the wallow, which was easier to regard even with icicles bending the reeds in the center. Then I unshipped the Deane-Adams and gave it to him along with my wallet and the badge of office. Water does them no good, holy or no.

FIVE

From the chill mountain air we passed through the open flap into a Turkish bath. Barrel stoves glowed at both ends of the tent, and with the rows of folding chairs all occupied and standees pressed together like kernels of corn at the back, the air was close and sultry and stank heavily of unwashed wool. Just inside the entrance an articulated skeleton in new overalls and a homespun shirt handed us each a slim hymnal bound in dirty green cloth and a sheet of coarse paper printed with smudged black letters:

DR. L. L. LITTLE'S TRAVELING TABERNACLE
Lawrence Lazarus Little, D.D., officiating
"A little leaven leaventh the whole lump."
— Galatians 5:6

Beneath was a calendar scheduling Little's travels throughout the spring and summer of the Year of Our Lord 1884.

"He has a following," Griffin said. "Some of the devoted trail him from place to place to hear the same sermons again and again. The theory seems to be that the more you're preached at, the holier your glow in the eyes of God. Watch."

The man Little was short but disproportionately wide through the trunk, an oak barrel on squat legs with long arms furred from the backs of his hands to the insides of his elbows, where the roll of his striped shirtsleeves prevented me from seeing how far up the hair grew; the fact that it sprouted again from his spread collar and tangled with his beard suggested he'd resemble a baboon when stripped. As we watched, he made his way down the aisle between the rows of chairs and penetrated the rows themselves, snatching sweaty sheets of paper from hands thrust at him, marking them with a stump of orange pencil, and returning them. "Bless you, brother, bless you, sister, bless you, child." The rolling voice spread benediction like a honey wagon.

Griffin shouted into my ear; the din of voices calling for Little's attention was palpable. "He scratches his initials beside the present location on the programme, like a conductor punching tickets. All you need do to pass through the heavenly gate is present it with all the places marked off. That's the assumption, in any case. He's far too clever to suggest it himself."

I said nothing, sparing my throat. I'd seen Edwin Booth signing autographs for a similarly frantic mob outside a theater in St. Louis. The spectacle of a man of the cloth being treated the same as a celebrated actor was new in my experience.

Eventually — to mortal groans from those clamoring in the back rows — the minister broke off his pilgrimage and trotted back up the aisle to a low platform erected of green lumber at the front of the tent, illuminated by a pair of barn lanterns strung from poles. Gripping a hymnal in one thistled fist he bade the congregation turn to page forty-three. Griffin nudged me and we sang, "Father, We Come to Thee," with Little's massy bass soaring above all. When the last straggler finished, he exchanged the hymnal for a much larger book resting on a straightback chair missing a rung and held the object high above his head. It was a Montgomery Ward & Co. catalogue, bound in blue paper with an engraving of the firm's Chicago headquarters on the front.

Knowing laughter greeted this gesture, as at the appearance of a favorite comic act.

"Satan's wish book," Griffin said; "this is a masterpiece."

I glanced at his clean profile, dry as flax in the sodden heat. I couldn't tell if he was being ironic.

"I see by your reaction you're all familiar with this object," Little said, beginning quietly; for with hasty shushings the crowd had fallen silent but for the odd nervous cough. "It is a miracle of our century: three hundred pages of text and lifelike illustrations offering more than thirty thousand items of merchandise for sale at competitive prices, from a sterling silver button hook for ninety-eight cents to a parlor grand piano for ninety-eight dollars, not including shipping and handling." (Laughter.) "It is possible, thanks to the foresight and American-style enterprise of Mr. Aaron Montgomery Ward of Chicago, Illinois, to purchase a heavy three-seat full platform wagon, a suit of clothes, a Remington New Model double-barrel shotgun, and seventy-two dozen shirt buttons without stirring from the chair beside your hearth. A wish book, my dear late wife called it." (Sympathetic murmurs.) "In short, my friends, there is nothing worldly that a man or woman with the necessary wherewithal may not obtain without so much as changing from a pair of comfortable house slippers into street shoes." (Nods and glances.) "We are fortunate, you and I, to live in such a society."

WHAM! With a sudden arcing flash of his arm, he cast the heavy volume to the floorboards at his feet. Even those who obviously had been witness to the same action on previous occasions jumped in their seats; the stout middle-aged woman standing next to me grasped my upper arm, letting go with a hurried whisper of apology. I said something polite back. I was somewhat shaken myself.

"There is another kind of wish book, my friends; and I do not refer to competing sources issued by Mr. Ward's Johnny-come-lately colleagues back East, but to the temptations stocked by our Savior's rival down South." (Uneasy chuckles.) "Mind you, Satan's wish book is not comprised of paper and ink. The text and illustrations are written in fire and blood, and the prices are kept secret until the bill comes due. It is issued by the old established concern of Pride, Lust, Covetousness, Wrath, Gluttony, Envy, and Sloth, and it is available on any public street corner for the unwary to browse at leisure.

"The greedy man who would fill his purse with gold while his neighbor goes hungry shall, when the creditor calls, be fitted with a pack containing four hundred times four hundred troy ounces to bear upon his back four hundred times four hundred miles, and four hundred times four hundred more, until the end of all things;

"The vain woman whose waist cannot be made too small that she may corrupt weak men shall, when the creditor calls, don a corset fashioned from barbed wire, a strand wound round a wheel, and that wheel spun, constricting her middle and forcing her innards into her limbs through eternity;

"The lazy man who lingers abed, neglecting the Lord's honest labor, shall, when the creditor calls, be nailed to a cot of hard rock maple and grow running sores of everlasting agony;

"The satyr who defiles virgins shall, when the creditor calls, be flung among harpies and ravished with truncheons of iron heated red in the fires of the furnace;

"The child who covets his playmate's catapult, so that he would make away with it without asking leave, shall, when the creditor calls, be himself placed in a sling and shot into the devil's own dung heap, ever and anon;

"The wife of simple circumstances with a good and devoted husband, who looks with jealous eyes upon her neighbor's hired girl, shall, when the creditor calls, wait on torn hands and bleeding knees upon Beelzebub's slut, who spares not the scourge, until the oceans boil and the sun is like unto a lump of ice;

"Finally, the man who lays about his family with his fists when no fault is theirs shall, when the creditor calls, be made a bitten dog which is starved, and spat upon, and soils itself when kicked, and wallows in its unholy filth until Saint Peter whistles.

"These are the prices demanded for the wares advertised in Satan's wish book: everlasting misery, eternal pain, humiliation without end. Let it never be said that the old established concern of Pride, Lust, Covetousness, Wrath, Gluttony, Envy, and Sloth failed to provide full customer satisfaction.

"Turn now to page ninety-eight."

We were halfway through "Memories of Galilee" before anyone at ground level could direct enough attention to the lyrics to give them conviction, such was the effect of the sermon. Little himself, by going straight to the hymn without pausing, appeared to hold any sort of reaction in small regard. It was grand showmanship; he might have been preaching to none but himself. The impression was of a man who cared less for personal glory than for his responsibility to his master. Few actors would have taken the chance, and no politician.

I said something along those lines to Griffin after the song ended. He nodded without turning his head. "It's like needing perfect pitch to sing deliberately off-key. Only a man who's passionately in love with himself could manage to appear so humble."

He asked what I'd thought of the sermon. I said, "It's just about the crudest thing I ever heard, but I was sorry when it ended."

"It's requested more often than his 'Express Train to Hell.' He's in danger of wearing it out. I don't believe he's changed a word in six years."

"I doubt I can touch it, even if I took it for myself."

"Don't try. What works under canvas won't play under board-and-batten. These people come expecting a bonfire, not a hearth at which to warm their hands."

"Then why did you bring me, apart from the baptism? Or is that the only reason?"

"You could be baptized in any place of worship, although I concede that doing so under less than ideal conditions appealed to me as punishment for your procrastination. I wanted you to see at firsthand that it's possible for a man who has no faith to inspire belief in others. I hardly expect you to rise to Lawrence Little's station, but had you not seen him in full cry, your doubts might have condemned you to failure."

"Little's a charlatan?" We'd been conversing in murmurs; I dropped mine to a whisper. The stout woman next to me was sending scowls my way.

"He didn't start out a fraud or he'd never have been ordained. However, I know when bombast has taken the place of devotion. He's been making that substitution as long as I've been attending his circus."

"It seemed genuine to me."

"That's because you have not stood where he is standing, mouthing the words that come from your head and not your heart."

Just then the collection plate came around. It was a hammered copper bowl with wooden handles. When we finished contributing and passed it on, the set of Griffin's jaw told me that path of conversation was closed.

At length the services ended and the baptisms began. A flap of canvas had been stitched to either side of the tent at the ends of the platform to create makeshift dressing rooms for men and women, and I joined a line. Griffin touched my arm. "You needn't. There are more accommodating places."

"It's hot as hell anyway," I said.

"That's the intention."

When my turn came I changed into a loose gown of unbleached muslin that reached to my ankles and gave my feet to a shapeless pair of shoes made from stiff uncured cowhide, with inner soles that felt like corrugated iron. I had my choice from a stack of gowns on a hewn bench and rows of footwear that looked uniformly uninviting, for the nippy weather outside had discouraged the less committed. I folded my clothes, put them and my boots in Griffin's hands for safekeeping, and went out to join one of two lines separated by gender marching toward the wallow. At first, the cold air felt good on my parboiled face, but as we shuffled along in half time to the congregation singing, "Jesus Wash Me," the sweat on my body seemed to form a jacket of ice. By the time we reached the edge of the water I was shivering and my feet felt like flagstones.

Brother Dismas, as I'd heard Little address the bald-headed beanpole who'd greeted us inside the tent, had shed his shirt and overalls for a gown and waded out to the middle without so much as a woof when the cold water came into contact with his testicles; his breath smoked in the air. Dr. Little meanwhile stood on dry land waving a brown-backed Bible and leading the chorus of hallelujahs that greeted each immersion. He was so enthusiastic, roaring in that voice so thoroughly cured in the barrel of his chest, that no one seemed to notice or mind that he never got his feet wet. I began to think that Griffin was right about him.

The water stung like needles when I went in, but as I pressed on, fighting to keep the gown from billowing and giving the parishioners more of a revelation than they'd come for, it clamped my legs in a vice that choked off all feeling. When I was crotch-deep, it pushed in with a surge that tore an oath from me, but if anyone heard it he must have thought I was overcome with rapture, because the reverend doctor went on encouraging the people still in line and didn't call down the lightning.

The good brother, who as far as I could tell was entirely hairless, with no sign that a razor had ever touched his bunched chin and sallow cheeks or had need to, laid a hand like a sash-weight on my shoulder and asked me, in a high-pitched voice that twanged like a bullet off a rock, if I renounced Satan and all his works.

I said, "Sure, but —" and then I was under; he'd slid his hand down to the small of my back, placed his other palm against my chest, and folded me backward, plunging me in and out in less than a second. When I got loose, spluttering and wiping water from my eyes, he grinned at me with two lines of pink gum. "But what?"

"Don't put me all the way under. I can't swim."

"Nor can buffler. That's why they don't go in more'n hock deep." He turned to the woman who'd waded in behind me and asked her where she stood on Satan and his works.

I foundered back toward shore, where Griffin waited with my clothes. He knew better than to say anything. In the cobbled-up men's dressing room I tossed the gown onto the soaking heap on the ground, wiped myself down with a towel damp from other bodies, and put myself back together. When I left the tent, Griffin was standing with Dr. Little, who'd rolled down his sleeves and put on a fine black broadcloth Prince Albert with velvet facings on the lapels. The bathing party had broken up.

"Father Griffin tells me you seek redemption." His grip was as strong as Brother Dismas', but not as skeletal. "You could not have chosen a better guide."

I looked at the former priest and got nothing back. We hadn't discussed secrecy, but he'd spent too much time in the confessional not to know a confidence when he was told one.

I said, "He's opened my eyes. That was a stirring sermon."

He chuckled. It was as if a steam thresher were starting up in his throat. He had a bulging forehead that made him look as if he was balding, but at closer range a crop of black hair as thick and coarse as the one that covered his body grew up from a straight line and swept back in an arc to the nape of his neck. His eyes were brown, mottled like river stones, and small, even teeth flashed in his beard. "Inspiration struck in an outhouse in Creede, where a torn copy of Ward's spring catalogue furnished an essential service. God never knocks, nor waits without."

Griffin shook his hand and wished him luck on the remainder of his tour. We left as a middle-aged couple stepped up to the head of the reception line. "Amazing," said Griffin. "He took in more today than Sacred

75

Hearts does in a month."

"Did you ask him if he needs a partner?"

He stopped walking and looked at me. "That is unkind."

Before I could respond he strode ahead. At the buggy he took my revolver and wallet and star from under the seat and gave them to me. We drove into town without a word. At the bottom of Catholic Hill he stopped to let me down and continued. There was no lesson that day.

Six

"Mrs. Blackthorne told me I'd find you here," I said. "I thought you didn't work on the Sabbath."

The Judge glared down at me. "I work every day. I'm not Pentecostal. It happens I report to chambers every other Sunday, when my parlor at home becomes the central headquarters of the Lewis and Clark County Book Club. Ostensibly they're discussing *The Adventures of Tom Sawyer*, but I doubt three of those esteemed ladies have read a line of Twain's. They gather to consume tea and thumping amounts of liverwurst and carve the ballocks off every married man in town."

Blackthorne stood on the top of a stepladder in the square, high-ceilinged room down the hall from his court where he retired to consider his rulings. He'd started with plenty of space, then crowded it with worktables, glazed book presses, books spread

77

open to passages of current interest, leather portfolios stuffed with reports and depositions, and old numbers of the *Montana Post* and the *Congressional Register,* in which he kept track of freebooters locally and in the U.S. Capitol. The only vacant seat was his own embossed-leather chair behind the big American walnut desk. The strategy was to discourage lengthy digressions by requiring gouty defense lawyers with big bellies and bad backs to stand throughout meetings. It seemed to work; they rarely ran longer than fifteen minutes and his court disposed of more cases per month than any other in the federal system.

He was in his waistcoat and shirtsleeves, removing dust from hefty legal volumes on his shelves with a deerskin rag. He never allowed the cleaners employed by the United States District Court to touch his personal library, which he'd assembled a piece at a time as he could afford it while clerking in a St. Louis firm and studying for the bar at night. They'd seen him through private practice, accompanied him to Washington during his lone term in the House of Representatives, and ridden in baggage cars, stagecoach luggage racks, the holds of steamboats, and on his own back when he'd crossed the prairie with his wife to take up his present post, and he wasn't about to trust them to any other hands.

He asked me how my education was progressing.

"You were right about Genesis," I said. "I made short work of it and have a dally around Exodus. Turns out the Bible's the easy part. Behaving as if I belonged in the same room with it's the part I'm having trouble with." I gave him an account of my morning.

Lawrence Little's chuckle and Blackthorne's shouldn't be referred to by the same term. The minister's was deep and plummy, the Judge's dry and sibilant, like a diamondback's buzz. "I wish I'd known. I'd have foregone the Reverend Clay's sermon on the destruction of Babylon and risked damnation just to see you tread water in a buffalo wallow in early spring."

"I'd respond to that, but I may need you to intercede for me with Griffin. If his door's not barred to me tomorrow I haven't got his measure."

"I doubt you have. No pleading on my part would improve your case. Griffin belongs to that stubborn cadre that's convinced I'm bound for hell. Every time I sentence a prisoner to hang I trespass upon the province of God."

"You might have let me know that before I went to his house carrying a letter of introduction signed by you."

"I had nothing to lose by being straight-forward, and with luck his cooperation to gain. He'd have known you came from me regardless. This way he's assured that no chicanery is involved."

"That won't help me now."

He twisted himself on the ladder, holding a tattered collection of Cicero's orations. The points of his brows were at their diabolical peak. "I honestly believe you're more self-obsessed than I. If he permitted you to cross his threshold on my behalf, condemned though I am, what makes you think he'll turn you away merely because you questioned his integrity?"

I saw there was no point in pursuing that line, so I chose another. "What made him break with the Church?"

"Ask him." He swept the rag across the untrimmed page edges and slid the book back into its slot.

"I did. He refused to answer."

"Then it's hardly my place to address the question."

"I didn't know you had a place."

He blew a dead bug off the top of *Principles Regarding the Division of Property in the State of Vermont, Vol. IX.* What system he used to categorize his library mystified me. "I keep an unruly pack of dogs to patrol a savage territory, Deputy," he said. "I hold the leash loose lest I break their spirit. Do not make the mistake of assuming I won't jerk it tight when one tries to urinate on me."

"I think you just did." I backed off. "He doesn't have a crucifix or a picture of Jesus anywhere in his house. If he's given up on faith, why do you suppose he's so concerned with how I represent it?"

"I wasn't aware he displayed no religious symbols in his home. I've never been invited." He sounded thoughtful.

"I'm trying to understand the man. I'll make an unconvincing minister if I don't."

"You'll make one regardless. But Ter Horst won't budge from his pious stance and you're the only other man available who can string ten words together without a spitoon handy. You're in the way of being me." The Vermont volume had a snug berth; he rammed it home with the heel of his hand and climbed down. Abusing books seemed to be a privilege of ownership, denied all others. He extended the same philosophy to the officers of his court.

He got rid of the deerskin and spent a full

minute brushing smears of dust from his waistcoat. "I daresay his complaint is not so much with belief as with the institution he served. No other concerns itself so completely with iconography. The absence of it from his own walls is a rebellion against Rome."

"What's his difference with the pope?"

"Chastity would be my guess. Celibacy. He opposes it."

"You're saying he threw the Church over for —"

"Hold your tongue on the Lord's day. As I understand the situation, it was a matter of romantic attraction, not lust."

"He fell in love with a woman? *Was* it a woman? I've heard stories."

"A woman was the reason, yes; but you've spent time with Griffin, and surely you've observed that whatever passion he has is reserved for the ethereal. The woman fell in love with him, and committed the blunder of confessing her temptations to her mother superior, who told the bishop, who cast her from the order. Griffin resigned in protest."

"She was a nun? What happened to her after that?"

"Her family disinherited her. Our society deals harshly with unmarried women of marked reputation with no one to support them and no skills with which to support themselves. A man like Eldred Griffin, having sacrificed his divine calling for the woman's sake, had no choice but to volunteer for the duty."

"Esther Griffin." I'd had it backwards, thinking she was the rock that kept him from collapsing under the weight of his own bitterness.

"Naturally, their betrothal lent credence to the rumors that her affections were requited, and that they had both sinned in the eyes of the Church. God spare us all from men who have the courage of their convictions."

He was one to talk. More than a few of his decisions had made enemies of powerful men he'd have been better served to pacify; letters to Congress had led to calls for impeachment. I said, "You know a lot about him for someone he hates."

"We've not met, and I doubt he'd confide in me if we had. A scandal limits itself to no particular denomination. The Reverend Clay is a gossip. If he weren't so useful as a source of intelligence, I might have converted to Lutheran years ago."

"It's no wonder he took it badly when I cast him in with Dr. Little. I'd have avoided it if you were half as forthcoming as Clay."

"You'd have found some other way to give offense. I suggest you make your peace. Your train pulls out in eight days."

Esther Griffin answered my knock Monday morning. She wore the same severe brown dress or one like it. "Mr. Griffin is ill. You must come back tomorrow." She started to close the door.

"Will it make a difference?"

She paused. "No."

"I didn't expect a lesson. I came to apologize."

"He said you would, after you spoke to your master. He won't accept."

"I want to do it anyway. If not to him, then to you."

She seemed to consider it. She had a kind face for all its lack of distinction. At length she moved aside to let me in.

The kitchen was her answer to her husband's study. In addition to the usual facilities for preparing meals and washing up after, it contained a bentwood rocker and a large sewing basket brimming over with spools of colored thread in a windowlit corner. A fancy bit of embroidery on white linen draped one arm of the chair. She went that way and twitched it so that the needlework didn't show, then moved a battered tea kettle from a trivet to the top of the wood range; apparently the silver set was for company, and I no longer qualified.

We sat at an oilcloth-covered table, where I pictured the couple sharing most meals, saving the simple dining room for guests. It wore a look of well-used comfort as opposed to the other, where even the hosts had seemed stiff and ill at ease; I was sure I'd been their first visitor in many a day.

She caught my glance straying toward the sewing corner. "I take in work sometimes. Eldred works hard, but there is only so much caretaking to be done in a small cemetery. We manage."

"I don't know when I've been in a place that felt so much like home."

"You're not married?"

I shook my head, and shook it again when she asked if it was because of the nature of my work. "Most of the deputies have wives. Sometimes I think they fished out the stream. It means a lot of nights spent alone waiting for bad news."

"Men give up so easily. But then it's always easy making the decision you've wanted to all along."

I wondered what was keeping that pot from coming to a boil.

"You mentioned an apology."

"I spoke out of turn yesterday. My work doesn't put me in contact with many honest men. You're not at it long before you begin to think everyone has his hand out. At the time I wasn't in possession of all the facts, but I knew by his reaction I'd made a huge mistake."

"The facts in regard to what?"

Her eyes were the color of her dress, and faintly cowlike. That made what was behind them a concealed weapon. I braced my hands on the table and sat back. "In regard to how he came to leave the Church."

"Judge Blackthorne told you? How — no, never mind. The clergy is worse than a house filled with old women." She got up to tend to the pot, which had come to a boil. She spooned tea from a square tin into two cups, poured in the steaming water, stirred, and returned to the table carrying a cup and saucer in each hand. When she was seated she said, "It's been so many years, and still they're talking about it. You'd think nothing else has ever happened in the Church."

"You don't have to talk about it. I wasn't asking."

"Who else is there to talk to? All our closest neighbors are dead. The Sisters of Mercy from Sacred Hearts pick up their habits and hurry past this house and cross themselves after. They won't forgive us for leaving and the Protestants we meet won't forgive us for having been in."

"That's part of the reason I've gone this long without religion."

"No one is without religion; not the gambler who credits his winning streak to luck or the woman who blames her dark star because her husband beats her. Have you ever connected a good or bad experience with timing?"

"I have, but I assumed the responsibility."

"I'm sure that's what you told yourself, but let us say you're right, and for whatever reason you've chosen to live without God. That's not the same as saying that God has had no influence upon you. The steps you've taken to avoid Him have altered your journey."

I drank tea. I was beginning to aquire a taste for it, or at least for the way she brewed it. I'd had camp coffee that was less strong. "I can see why your husband doesn't encourage these discussions."

"My mother superior shared the aversion. I was naïve. A convent is no place for a lively exchange of ideas. I believe now that if I had not made the mistake of confiding my inner feelings to her, she would have found some other way to dispose of me."

"Then you have no regrets?"

She curled both hands around her cup and looked at her reflection on the surface. "I regret daily that I didn't hold my tongue and let nature find another course, one that did not destroy Eldred's life."

"Does he look at it that way?"

She picked up her ears, motioning for silence. The residents of that house seemed superhumanly attuned to the sound of their names. The stairs creaked and in a moment Griffin entered the kitchen. When he saw me he stopped, although of course he had to have known I was there. The place was small and voices traveled, even if words didn't.

"Did you return his money?" he asked his wife.

"I did not. We've spent some, and it would be weeks before we could save enough to return it. And you agreed to provide the instruction Mr. Murdock requested."

"I changed my mind."

I started my speech of apology, but she interrupted me. "You made a bargain; but we'll overlook that. A partial education in the ways of the Lord is worse than none at all. He might take what he's learned and not knowing the rest twist it to suit selfish purposes. I've heard you say that a hundred times about these traveling opportunists."

"He thinks I'm one of them."

"He's spent most of his visit telling me he doesn't. If you hadn't fled into your burrow when he knocked at the door, he'd have told you."

"There's been entirely too much telling going on. You've been doing most of the talking."

"Our story is known, but it's been poorly told. Should our enemies' version be the only one anyone hears?"

I scraped my chair back and stood. "I should leave."

"You should come upstairs," Griffin said. "A kitchen is for filling your belly, not your head."

SEVEN

The programme accelerated from that hour. Griffin seemed suddenly conscious of the time constraint and sped through the less illuminating biblical passages, questioning me sharply on certain points without warning, a bushwhacking maneuver that caught me unprepared the first time, but not again. His Church was founded on the New Testament, and lest the apostles be slighted for the sake of catching a train, we studied them between First and Second Kings. Infrequently he elaborated on the text, providing extraneous but revealing detail on the structure of the Roman legions and farming methods under the pharaohs of Egypt. His ragtag library was as heavy on history as it was light on theology; his massive Bible was the only religious authority in the room apart from himself. Arguments in print appeared to put him off as much as dissent from his wife, whom experience had taught him to defer to early and avoid a long and pointless discussion with the same result. He would not defer to rival philosophers.

One morning, near enough to date of departure to spoil my concentration with thoughts of linen and train changes, he marked his place in Deuteronomy with his bit of strop and shut the book with a thump. "How much experience have you had with speaking in public?"

"I've given manhunting parties their charges in town squares from here to California," I said.

"Bawling like a master sergeant and preaching to the faithful do not belong to the same world, particularly in a proper house of worship. You must speak as if you were alone with one parishioner, yet be heard as clearly in the rear pew as in the front. That last is important. People who sit in front are already disposed to pay close attention. It's the stragglers who perch near the door you must capture. They will fly at the first dry rustle."

"I'll try to get in some practice."

"What will you speak about?"

"I don't figure I can go wrong with 'Love thy Neighbor' and 'Stay Out of Hell.' "

He pulled his lips away from his teeth. I think they were false — no set ever grew so evenly or stayed so white — but the work-manship was superior to Judge Black-thorne's, which fit him so uncomfortably he wore them only on public occasions. He must have gone to a Catholic dentist while still a priest. "Why do you suppose most people go to church?"

The answer was too obvious for it to be anything but a trick question, but I've never learned anything by avoiding a trick. "To pray."

"They can do that at home. Some attend out of fear of damnation, or love of salva-tion, or because their friends and family expect them to, or to win public office, or to drum up business; back East, they would be the majority. Here on the frontier, most people surrender their one day of rest to be entertained. Be truthful. When you went in to hear Lawrence Little, did you expect to enjoy the experience?"

"No. I expected to be bored to my boots, then get frostbite in a buffalo wallow."

"I'd suspected there was truth in the compliment you paid him. Preposterous and blatant as it is, his Sunday-school-simpleton picture of hell is what puts them on their feet and brings back return custom-ers who know the text by heart. Some of those who were baptized with you had already been in ponds and springs and swollen streams where the Traveling Tabernacle has stopped in the past. The blessing does not wear out or expire; renewal is not necessary. They wanted to be part of the show. Very few seriously believe they're in danger of being condemned perpetually. Those who do are not so simple as to accept Little's parable of the torturous corset as punishment for vanity. It's theater, and only a fool thinks Ophelia is going barking mad before his eyes. The rest do insist that the *performer* believes, or produces a reasonably convincing counterfeit, preferably with Roman candles or some substitute. If all they wanted was the Golden Rule, they would stay home and read Matthew."

"You're forgetting I'm going there to make arrests, not fill the collection plate."

"And when half your congregation stays home the second Sunday, who's to tell you whom to arrest? Barren soil yields dust."

I surrendered the point. "I'd planned to read straight from Scripture, but you've shot that down."

"You're supposed to interpret it, not parrot it. A casual familiarity with the statutes won't win a legal case or we'd not need lawyers who are themselves entertainers." He twisted to face his writing table and ransacked the heap of books and documents on top until he drew out a bundle of papers as thick as a brand book, bound lengthwise and sidewise with dirty cord. The edges were ragged and molting. They appeared to have been chewed by mice: *Church mice,* I thought, and surprised myself by feeling shame for thinking it. I wondered if piety was contagious.

I took the bundle, shedding paper flakes all over my lap. It was heavier than my own Bible and smelled like silage.

"My sermons," he said. "Call it 'The Gospel According to Griffin' if you like. You'll need to make them your own. I wrote them with a cadence in mind that was comfortable to me, but no two musicians play the same tune the same way. I expect them back. I'd almost sooner part with Esther."

Was there a flat note of insincerity in his *almost?* I asked myself if he didn't share his wife's regret. "Thank you. I doubt I'll be able to copy out many of them before I leave."

"I'm suggesting you take them with you. Yours is not a tent show. It may be months before you finish your mission. Your audience will expect something fresh each week."

"Are you sure you want to trust me with them? I've a habit of traveling light, with nothing I can't bring myself to abandon if the hunt goes the other way."

"I haven't decided to trust you with them yet. I'll reserve judgment until I've heard you read one in church. I've persuaded Father Medavoy to lend us the use of Sacred Hearts tomorrow morning. No services are scheduled that day. We'll have the place to ourselves and the odd sparrow."

"That's cutting it close. My train's Saturday. We're not halfway through the Bible."

"The seminaries are turning out graduates with a half knowledge of the Bible at best, and there are pastors who've forgotten more than that but continue to drift along on the same dogma they've been preaching for fifty years. As it stands, you know more than most of those who will come to you for spiritual aid, and it hasn't escaped my notice that you have the gift of blarney. My mother's people were Irish; I failed to inherit, but I have a healthy respect for it. I'm confident you'll find a way to fill the gap."

"I can't help but suspect you're giving me up as a lost cause."

"I resent the implication. I collect my pay for resodding sunken graves with my chin high, and if I thought I had shorted Judge Blackthorne in any way, I would return his gold if it meant working for Methodists to make up the difference."

I didn't know what to say to that, whether to ask why pulling weeds for the Methodist Church was more demanding than performing similar work for Sacred Hearts. Democrats vs. Republicans was enough of a closed door without pondering the politics of prayer. What I came up with was, "What if you don't like what you hear tomorrow morning? If I get a failing grade, do I get to stay home?"

"I've not met your employer, but based on what I've heard of his methods, he'll toss you into the furnace regardless of anything I might say. I seek merely to satisfy myself that I've done all I can in two weeks that can be expected of mortal man when faith is involved. If in my heart I cannot accept that I am doing other than releasing yet another profanity upon the land, I will beg your Judge on my knees to send me in your place."

"He'd never agree to that. It would be a death sentence."

"Just so."

A squeak from the floor below told me that Esther Griffin had opened the damper in the stovepipe to prepare noon dinner. I'd come to know the house like none I'd lived in since my father's dugout in the mountains, and the thought that I would soon leave it, with no good excuse to come back, put the cold lump of homesickness deep in my belly.

"I can't get the straight of you," I said. "How can you still be so devoted to God after He treated you as He has?"

He showed surprise for the first time since we'd met, and it was a testimony to how well I'd come to know him that I recognized it; the deep latitudinal lines that were so much a part of his forehead disappeared, the skin drawn taut by the movement of his scalp. It was a shape-shifting moment.

"God never deserted me," he said. "In return for my earthly disgrace He gave me Esther. It's a debt I can never repay. No other mortal in Creation has been permitted to take an angel unto himself."

"Have you said as much to Esther?"

"It would be superfluous. Angels know they're angels."

I didn't wander any deeper into country where I had no jurisdiction. He might have been able to address a churchful of people as if he were talking to one, but when it was just one he was wretched.

Our session ended and I went back to my room to look through the bundle. The undated pages were tanned and brittle and threatened to fall apart at the folds when I cut the cord. He'd filled them with a bold round hand with few cross-outs and corrections and not a single blot. At first it seemed like poetry and I nearly gave up because I can't recite verse without sounding like a bored railroad conductor announcing the next stop, but when I tried one there in the privacy of my own quarters it came as easily as breathing. He'd found the difference between writing to be read and writing to be heard; what looked like broken pieces of sentences to the eye sounded like natural conversation when read aloud. Not surprisingly, because the Christian God is not the wrathful ogre of the Old Testament, there was little about flames that burned without consuming and much about forgiveness and mercy; but Eldred Griffin's Jesus was not the bearded lady I'd seen in picture books and in pasteboard frames on people's walls. Virile, decisive, and committed, his was the authority that hurled the money changers out of the temple and told the devil to go to hell with his kingdoms of gold. He reminded me of Griffin himself, who if he had not remade God in his own image had certainly placed his stamp upon Him.

I made my selection finally, and from sundown to well past midnight sat at the narrow drop-front desk that came with the room, transcribing the text onto a separate sheet, making small changes that suited my inferior breath control, and burning the phrases deep into my memory until my eyes gave out and I couldn't turn up the lamp any more without smudging the glass chimney. I retired then and spent the rest of the dark hours dreaming I stood naked at the pulpit before pews packed with my enemies. It made for a full house.

Griffin greeted me at the door of the Cathedral of the Sacred Hearts of Jesus and Mary and remarked that I hadn't slept well. I held up my pages of notes by way of answer.

"You're prepared, then. I expect much."

Thus pressed, I crossed the cavernous room up the center aisle, with the sensation that I was following the echo of my footsteps rather than the reverse. The morning sun leaning in through the tall stained-glass windows cast colored reflections on the oiled pews, and the sparrows Griffin had predicted fluttered between the rafters, looking for a place to perch and take in the performance. The place smelled of candle wax and varnish.

I mounted the steps to the pulpit. Father Medavoy, the pastor, was tall, and had directed a volunteer to raise it with planks for his comfort, bringing it to the top of my sternum. I felt like an altar boy serving out some kind of humiliating punishment. Griffin, no help, took a seat in the very back, nearly out of pistol range from where I stood arranging my pages on a slantboard with a pencil rail at the base.

I cleared my throat and began.

"Louder!"

I started again, raising my voice.

"Louder!"

I shouted.

"Not so loud! It's a sermon, not a roll call."

I made two more tries before he fell silent long enough for me to get to the body of the text. It was a parable of his own creation, about a boy whose brother had died before he was born, and who through a misunderstanding thought him an angel, to whom he prayed for an end to his parents' grief. It was guaranteed to wring tears from listeners, but acting upon some instinct I kept them from my own voice. It ended with the parents on their knees embracing their only child.

Silence struck like a bell. Even the light hiss of air stirring in the barnlike room had stopped. After a second (minute?) or two I began to hope I'd lost my hearing.

"Why did you pause before the last line?" Griffin asked then, and the air resumed stirring. Outside the nearest window a creaking carriage, which had halted in its tracks, started moving again.

"I thought it needed a running start."

"Leaps of faith don't. Why were you not moved by the tale?"

"I was, although I didn't expect to be when it started."

"I saw no tears and heard no sobs."

"I practiced to eliminate them. I heard somewhere that a humorous story sacrifices its effect when the speaker laughs. I gambled that the same holds true when the story's tragic."

"Indeed." Silence set back in. "Well, you won your gamble. You must let the listener draw from his own well. Why did you look up so seldom? Did you not commit your text to memory?"

"I did, but I got nervous."

"A display of fear is a confession of sin. You must speak as if each word has just occurred to you, and engage the eye of some random member of the audience. If he appears hostile, challenge him with your gaze to find fault with your point. If friendly, invite him into your exclusive tabernacle as One Who Understands. Leave the sheets at home and banish the temptation to steal a look."

I knew I could never do that, any more than I could go into a fight unarmed. "Am I as bad as all that?"

"I've heard worse right where you're standing. Do not interpret that to mean I consider you any better than scarcely adequate. However, only Our Father can grow wings on a frog in a fortnight. Step down."

I did, and started down the aisle, my knees wobbling like a broken spoke now that the ordeal was over. As I neared his pew he slid out and gave me a parcel wrapped in brown paper tied with string. It was bigger than the bundle of sermons but much lighter. "From Esther."

I unwrapped a folded shirt made of good simple gray linen. At first glance it looked like ordinary homespun, but the seams were double-stitched with uncommon skill. It was work more than worthy of a woman who took in sewing simply to help with the household accounts.

Such garments have attached collars generally, but a heavily starched white band had been fastened to it with studs. It was a preacher's clerical collar. I touched it. I'd never felt one.

"My last," Griffin said. "I thought I'd thrown them all out, but she said I overlooked this one, which happened to be my best. I suspect she squirreled it away."

The gift touched me. I thought I'd outgrown the emotion. "I'll try not to bring shame on it."

"It's blasphemous to promise miracles. I'll be satisfied if you don't get blood on it."

I thought of what he'd said the next day — my forty-third birthday — as I lay in a muck of dirt and dung waiting for a pair of my fellow pioneers to stir themselves to carry me to Dr. Alexander's office. I was saving my new shirt for the trip, and good job, because the one I had on was soaked through with blood.

At length I was collected and borne up the outside stairs to the little room above the hardware store, leaving behind the crowd that always gathers around medicine shows and shootings. Alexander, a wiry, excitable man of thirty, directed the volunteers to stretch me out on the cot and herded them outside. He locked the door, drew the window shade, and resumed his study of the *Herald* at his rolltop.

A moment later Judge Blackthorne came in from the private quarters in back. I was sitting now on the edge of the cot. He contemplated the stain on my shirt. "What did you use?"

"Calves' blood, from the meat shop. Matthews put it in a fish bladder. All I had to do was hang it around my neck under my shirt and give it a smack when I heard the shot."

"He'll keep silent?"

"He'd better. Half his business comes from the jail, and there are other markets in town. Where's Bullard?" Roy Bullard was the mail robber who was supposed to have been gunning for me.

"California, last I heard. That was Deputy Leffler behind the Winchester. He's a crack shot."

"He's too confident. The slug took a piece out of a porch post not two feet away. If he misjudged the wind, or I dove the wrong way, that's money wasted getting Griffin to make me a reformed character."

"It had to look convincing, and blank cartridges lack the authoritative report of a live round. We discussed all this. You need to be dead on the off chance someone recognizes you in Texas. The more witnesses the better, to make him doubt his own suspicions."

"If you wanted to make it credible you should have had ten men ambush me with shotguns."

"You've been reading dime novels about your exploits when you should have been studying Holy Writ." He unslung his watch and sprang the lid. "Ten minutes from now, the doctor will announce your demise to your admirers outside."

"Twenty," put in Alexander. "I have a reputation as well."

"Twenty it is. You will then be carried under cover of a sheet to Wilson's New Method Undertaking Parlor, where you will spend the next eighteen hours out of sight; the jail does business with Wilson as well, so his discretion is reasonably assured."

"*Where* out of sight?"

"The preparation room. I'm told there are no corpses there at present, but should the situation change, your natural stoic disposition will see you through any discomfort. I'm scheduling your services for tomorrow morning at nine: closed coffin, of course. By then you'll be in the baggage car of the eight-forty to Denver. After you change trains, you can ride to Amarillo with the rest of the human cargo, under the name

Sebastian. Brother Bernard Sebastian of the Church of Evangelical Truth."

My lips twisted. I couldn't help it. "Saint Bernard?"

"Two saints, to be precise. Double the benediction."

"Your faith in numbers is misplaced. You've already dealt too many in on the hand."

"Death is a committee affair; but we must trust the cards. Rumors fuel the West. The deceased walk, the quick are dead. Last month Jesse James was seen coming out of an ice cream parlor in Chicago, and he's been worm fodder for two years. No one eats what's set before him without seasoning it heavily with irony. A bit of gaseous legend can only contribute to verisimilitude."

"I don't know that word, but if it means going off half-cocked, I agree with it."

He traded his watch for a thick wallet and held it out. I took it from habit; people had been giving me things for days. It was made of shoddy brown leather, fraying through at the fold. "Banknotes?"

"Personal effects: a letter from the fictitious Sebastian's dear dead mother, scribbled accounts of travel expenses, receipts for provisions, the usual mortal debris. They'll address questions about your identity. The devil is in the details." He smiled, lips tight.

■ ■ ■ ■

II
THE PARABLE OF THE PILGRIM

■ ■ ■ ■

EIGHT

As it happened, Bucephalus Wilson, the undertaker, had a rush job, to improve the complexion of an old man who'd died of jaundice, and do it in time to ship him to Denver in the same baggage car Blackthorne had reserved for me. Since I had nothing better to do while waiting I helped out by handing things to Wilson, chiefly a pot of aluminum paste he applied as a sort of primer and a tin of pink powder to lend his customer the glow of health. It was interesting work, and the undertaker was good company, as might be expected since the Judge's deputies brought him so much business.

I won't dwell on that cold lonely ride across the High Plains, because it's as boring to tell as it was to experience. The old man's coffin gave me a seat, and I had a railroad lantern to warm my hands over until a porter came to tell me to put it out.

A clerk had arranged to have my valise carried aboard, so I had my extra suit coat to keep me from freezing. I'd bought it, with black trousers to match, from a back room of the Drew Emporium where reclaimed and mended clothing sold for poverty prices. The coat was big enough to hide my revolver and shabby enough for a minister who survived on Christian charity.

As far as the train personnel were concerned I'd requested the windowless coach to flee an angry wife; boarding early under cover of darkness supported the story. I doubt they believed a word of it, but enough money had changed hands to keep their curiosity in check. In any case they didn't know where I was going after Denver, and they saw so much in the course of a working day to lower their opinion of the human race the odds were they forgot about me as soon as they finished unloading.

I didn't like the odds. A secret parsed more than two ways is like three men on one horse: You know it will collapse, but you're not sure when. But that was an inept comparison, because I was the only one in danger of falling. In Denver I went to the water closet three times to make sure I wasn't being followed. The other people waiting in the station looked at me sympathetically. It was obvious to them I had a medical problem.

It's a shuddery stretch from the Rockies to the desert Southwest, but the chair car felt like a private Pullman after the journey in baggage. I sank with a sigh of pleasure into horse hair stuffing that had shifted to accommodate backsides shaped very differently from mine and made myself intimate with the contents of Brother Bernard's wallet, and with the fabled Mr. Sebastian himself.

I sensed the Judge's devious hand behind the letter from Sebastian's mother, with perhaps Mrs. Blackthorne's gentler touch in the tender parts. I'd never seen a sample of her penmanship, but there was a womanly swoop in the tails and capitals, and I doubted anyone in the ruthlessly masculine organization of the Helena federal court could have managed the endearing phrases it helped form. In between, a more calculating mind had leavened in information that provided the bearer with both a history and an ironclad fence to prevent anyone from confirming or discounting it.

It was on the order of an expression of maternal gratitude and a helpful guide through the changeable landscape of a difficult world. Cleverly, Blackthorne had inserted pertinent details that explained how Sebastian had been thrust into it full-grown. Mother Sebastian, it seemed, had composed the letter to be discovered by her son among her personal effects, and read after her death. His father had been dead for many years. In his absence, young Sebastian had cared for his invalid mother in a house belonging to a Mrs. Brown in or near Denver. The father, a Church deacon, had tutored him in religion, so there was no reason to advise him about gentlemanly conduct once he was on his own, but the old lady took care to instruct her son on certain practical matters to ease his entry into the society of man. I learned from it how to save money, what to look for in a buggy horse, the importance of choosing friends cautiously, and the sort of woman to avoid. I'd have profited from knowing the first three twenty years ago, but I doubt I'd have paid much attention to the last even then. Perfidious women are an education all by themselves.

It was a remarkable document. I got lost in it, truth to tell, and found myself picturing an authentic Bernard Sebastian somewhere out there, born of an ailing mother rich in the wisdom of her years. It couldn't have been all fabrication. There was a rumor (which the Judge would have slashed to bits if it were ever mentioned in his presence) that the Blackthornes had lost a child in infancy years before they came to Montana Territory. Now I saw foundation in it. These were lessons intended for a youth who hadn't lived long enough to benefit from them. On the other hand, Mrs. Blackthorne was a great reader of novels, the chair-woman of a book club, and never missed the first night of a new production at the Ming Opera House, so I might have been wasting compassion on nothing more poi-gnant than a lively sense of theater.

Purely as an instrument of my mission, it was expert craftsmanship. A place the size of Denver and its environs would be too thick in "Mrs. Browns" to encourage anyone to look up Sebastian's former landlady, and the name of the church where his father had served as a lay preacher wasn't mentioned; the city had dozens. A man of middle age seeking a pulpit in Texas could not have answered queries into his experience better than to claim he'd spent the last couple of de cades nursing a bedridden patient and studying the Bible. Such exemplary sacrifice established him as a righteous man, and having a deacon for a sire entitled him to semiprofessional status at least. Mistakes made in front of the congregation would be assigned to his lack of an opportunity to practice what he'd learned in public.

So the old bastard was anticipating I'd fall on my face. As was I, but my pride was stung. All right, it's a sin, and so is wrath. I wanted to wring his neck.

I put back the letter and examined the rest. Someone familiar with my expense vouchers had come disturbingly close to duplicating my hand in the little writing block where Sebastian kept track of his travel budget. It, and what looked like a complete collection of receipts for possibles that he might need on the road, led me to believe that Brother Bernard was close with a buck, which befit a pilgrim of small means, but it was overdone. Devotion is difficult enough to manufacture without having to try to be a prig as well. I threw the receipts out the window.

I learned from a telegram, composed in Owen, Texas, and sent through Wichita Falls by way of the Overland, that Sebastian's request for a pastorship had been accepted "on approval" by a director with the First Unitarian Church who went by the intriguing name of "R. Freemason." The lack of an outright commitment indicated there were concerns about my being an evangelist.

Communication by telegraph meant that a court contact in Denver had wired the original petition, and sent the response to Helena.

Stuck in the fold of the wallet I found a stiff rectangle about the size of a penny stamp: an orange and wrinkled tintype of a sheep-faced woman in her fifties, a son's only likeness of his sainted mother. I wondered who she was really.

Blackthorne had thought of everything. He'd gone to a deal of trouble to place me in the thick of a robbery investigation in someone else's jurisdiction. I couldn't believe his only motive was to run the gang to ground in Texas on the slim chance that if it were left unfettered it might shift its activities to Montana Territory.

Taking this assignment was like sitting in on a poker game where the dealer made up all the rules. I wouldn't mind losing so much as not knowing why. But if I'd turned it down he'd have found something worse. That was the thing about the frontier: There was always something worse.

Texas doesn't belong in the same sentence with the place I considered home, or for that matter on the same continent. As far as I was concerned it had broken off from southern Spain or northern Africa, blown about for a while to dry out some more like a dead cottonwood leaf, and come to rest a day's ride from the border of Colorado, where at least winter had the good manners to pause for conversation before heading north. To get there from where I'd started you had to cross the Cimmaron Strip: two hundred square miles of rugged land that was supposed to belong to the Indian Nations, but which had been overlooked when the territorial lines were drawn, leaving a slot-shaped hole in America where road agents scuttled like roaches when dawn broke. That was where mine would head if I put my foot wrong in Owen, and if I were reckless enough to follow them there, Brother Bernard would be dead before his first birthday. I'd taken the oath expecting to die in its honor, but dying twice in one season wasn't in it.

At Colorado Springs, our last stop in civilization, the greeters and loafers on the platform wore scarves and heavy pullovers and moved in close to warm themselves in the steam when the train braked. In Texas a couple of hours later, when we stopped to let off passengers and take on water, they wore loose cotton, sweat through under the arms, and stepped back to escape the moist heat. By then I'd shrugged out of my heavy preacher's weeds and pushed up the window against the furnace blast of wind scraping sand from Arizona Territory, which was the only place I'd spent time where you closed up the house to keep the heat out, and the only place that had somewhere to dump the heat it couldn't handle.

Somewhere being Texas.

Put that together with arid gusts that rocked the stationary cars like Confederate grapeshot, and you can begin to understand the conditions in panhandle country. No other spot on the map was better named, with the possible exception of the Dead Sea. You know that if you've ever tried to lift a heated skillet by its handle without first wrapping a rag around it. Sitting in that close coach, waiting for the train to pull out and fanning myself with Brother Bernard's wallet, I watched a stove-in galvanized bucket bounding across the prairie like a spooked antelope and wondered where it would stop this side of Arkansas, or if barring a fence or a corn rick or a sedentary hog, it would clatter through North Carolina, cross the Atlantic and the Gobi Desert, and make its way around the world back to that same patch of dead earth. That was one sophisticated bucket. I'd have gone out to intercept it, if for no other reason than that a rude receptacle of water shouldn't be more well-traveled than I, if I weren't afraid the train would leave me behind with the gilas and roadrunners.

That was my objection to Texas and its featureless landscape. I liked mountains on one side, waving grass on the other, and here and there a saloon or a brothel or even a bank or post office to interrupt the monotony, but the whole state was flat enough to duck under a fence. I'd ridden far for the court and had seen both extremes, cities of brick and stone decked out in coats of soot and spreading acres empty to the horizon. I wanted something in between, with an open window handy in case I changed my mind.

Then there were the Texans themselves; but more about them later.

I wasn't looking forward to crossing the same country again by horse. I'd overshot my destination for practical reasons and also for duty. There was as yet no rail line to Owen or anywhere within a full canteen of it, and I had a Ranger station to report to at end of track before I set out. Ever since he'd lost two deputies in a misunderstanding in old Mexico, Blackthorne had been a stickler about checking in with local authority. The federales had taken the bigger hit, but he'd just escaped congressional censure over the affair, and the Mexican major in charge had been stood up against a wall in Mexico City.

As we resumed rolling, a man and woman entered the car through the connecting door, balancing themselves against the sway with the support of the seats and the weight of their bags. They were both dressed for town, the woman in tightly woven tweeds as armor against cinders, and I thought they were together, but after the man hoisted her portmanteau into the overhead rack, she thanked him and they sat down on opposite sides of the aisle, she to gaze out at the scenery, such as it was, he to open a copy of *The Fort Worth Gazette* and lose himself in the gray columns.

That was the payload, not counting freight, and it didn't say much in favor of where we were heading. I could only hope I could at least get drunk there.

I wished I'd bought a paper while we were stopped. I didn't care what was going on in Fort Worth, and there was never anything for me in the telegraph columns from New York and Washington, but I'd forgotten to bring a deck of cards and that last leg promised even less in the way of diversion than all those that had preceded it. I opened my Bible to Ecclesiastes. The Preacher strummed the same three notes, time and oppression and no new thing under the sun; he must've taken the same trip. I dozed, and woke, and saw nothing had changed outside, not even a shadow to tell me how long I'd slept. The woman had given it up to knit and the man was snoring with his *Gazette* spread over his face.

In due course we passed a pile of broken crates and empty lard cans that meant a settlement coming up. An ancient conductor with railroad-issue bad feet and a pair of moustaches the size of saddle pouches hobbled down the aisle shouting, "Wichita Falls," as if it were the first circle of hell.

Slowing, we slid through a neighborhood of chalk-gray houses and drew up alongside a station bright with fresh paint. I took my bones out of the seat and scooped my valise from the rack. "Where's the nearest place to get a steak and a bottle?"

The conductor's moustaches moved as he chewed. He parted them to squirt a muddy stream at the cuspidor at my feet. "Kansas City."

NINE

Lone Star lore, which is what the rest of the country calls a barefaced lie, says the first owner of the site on the Wichita River won it in a poker game. The other version is it was part of a legitimate purchase of land certificates, but he must not have thought much of them because he put them away and forgot they existed. When the trunk was opened almost forty years later, mice and squirrels had eaten all the better prospects and Wichita Falls was what was left.

The crook who platted the tract drafted a nonexistent lake, cotton warehouses, and steamboats in quantity. None of those things ever materialized, and by the time the town had a church and a post office and a public school even the falls had vanished, pounded flat by the relentless water. After that it might have followed a hundred other Western towns into oblivion but for a land-concession deal with the Fort Worth &

Denver Railway Company that amounted to property confiscation in return for a spur line. Behind the tracks came the station, a shingle and sorghum mill, a lumberyard, a general store, and promotion to county seat.

All this had happened in five years. When I first saw it, the place was built of loblolly pine shipped in from the East with no foundation between it and the natural limestone and smelled of sawdust and turpentine; when the wind shifted crossways the sting made your eyes water. All it took was a flake of hot ash from a pipe or a spark from a train wheel to wipe it out in four hours.

Except, of course, for the rails. The robber barons had stitched up the continent with steel thread that will still be there after the next great flood.

The station agent, a short twist of hickory with handlebars that extended past his shoulders, told me I could find Captain Jordan of the Texas Rangers in the back of the post office. I asked him if there was a hotel in town. He shook his head and gave me a ticket for my valise.

"How many bags have you got waiting to be reclaimed?" I asked.

"Just the one."

The regional Texas Rangers headquarters

hung its shingle above a separate entrance to the post office, which was the only building in town flying the Stars and Stripes. I knocked, got a bark from inside, and opened the door on an office the size of a cloakroom. There was a plank floor without a rug, a barrel stove, a cot, the obligatory spitoon — pewter, with the initials of the Fort Worth & Denver Railway Company embossed on the flange around the top — a green-painted table, two chairs, a Windsor and a ladderback, and a male creature seated on the ladderback who might have been the twin of the station agent, left out in the weather. His handlebars were fair whereas the other's were brown and his hair had gone unbarbered long enough to curl back up toward the brim of his mottled pinch hat, but he had the same eyes like steel shot and hawk's-beak nose that looked as if it had been broken at birth.

He had a copy spread on the table of what looked like the same edition of *The Fort Worth Gazette* I'd seen aboard the train and was using a wooden yardstick and a clasp knife to cut a neat rectangle out of the lead column. He didn't glance up as I entered but told me to take a seat. He had a big voice for a small man; not as deep as Dr. Lawrence Lazarus Little's, but what it lacked in timbre it made up for in volume, with that burred edge that comes from shouting orders against the west Texas wind. I sat, and noticed that his yardstick was stenciled with the name of the Fort Worth & Denver Railway Company and that the knife he was using was the kind issued to porters to cut the tags off luggage and probably had the same legend printed on the handle. A panoramic photograph of two rows of Texas Rangers, one standing, one sitting cross-legged on the ground, all armed with pistols and carbines, hung crooked in a walnut frame on the wall behind his head. As far as I could tell, the railroad hadn't gotten around to slapping its brand on that.

He finished cutting, peeled up the rectangle, and spiked it on a spindle on a cast-iron base. Other cuttings, scraps of scribbled paper, and telegraph flimsies climbed halfway up the spindle.

I asked him if he'd been mentioned in the newspaper.

"Not me. The Rangers." He crumpled the rest and tossed it into an open crate in the corner by the Republic of Texas flag on a stand. "Every time we're in print I'm supposed to save it and send it on to San Antonio." He'd lowered his voice, but it still carried. I couldn't hear anything from the post office side, so the walls must have been stout. "That's what we do up here since we whipped the Comanches. All the men I need to keep the peace are down shooting greasers on the Rio Grande. Who the hell are you?"

"Are you Captain Jordan?"

"Would I be sitting in this shithouse if I wasn't?"

"Don't get your back up, Captain. The more people know I'm alive, the less chance I've got of staying that way." I showed him the star and the letter from Judge Black-thorne. His own star, which was nearly as plain as mine, hung on a pocket of his blue flannel shirt, with two inches of white union suit sticking out of the cuffs. He was one of those who believe in insulating themselves against the heat.

In his case it seemed to work. He wasn't sweating, and the room couldn't have been hotter if it had been built above a black-smith's forge. He looked well past fifty, but taking into account the oven conditions in that country he might have been ten years younger. He didn't wear spectacles and held the letter at normal length while reading.

He laid it down, fingered through the stack of papers on the spindle starting at the base, and tore one loose a third of the way up from the bottom, then smoothed it out beside the letter. He wasn't comparing the writing, because the second sheet was a telegram that had been taken down by a key operator in Wichita Falls. It was a carefully whittled message from Judge Blackthorne, who never spent a taxpayer's penny on unnecessary verbiage, asking him to cooperate with a visitor bearing a letter from him. Learning to read upside-down is useful in my work.

Jordan aimed a square-nailed thumb over his shoulder at the waste paper in the crate. "You're dead in today's *Gazette.*"

"In yesterday's *Independent,* too, up in Helena." I tried not to preen. Vanity's a stubborn sin to lick when you find out you're news so far outside your range.

"Anyone can write a letter. Got anything to prove you're who you say?"

"I left my commission behind. Traveling with the badge and letter was risky enough. I'll thank you to burn the letter and I'm putting the badge in your charge when I leave here."

He ruminated. Then he rolled onto one hip; to let wind, I thought, and in that thick air I came closer to panicking than I had since the Judge's sniper had shaved things so thin back home. Instead he hauled out a long-barreled converted Colt Paterson with a worn brown finish from a scabbard that went down into his back pocket, cocked it, and clunked it down on the table. "I'll have that pistol under your arm."

I was wearing the coat I'd had tailored to cover it, but he'd make it his business to know why I kept it on in the heat. I lifted the Deane-Adams clear, holding the butt between thumb and forefinger like a dead fish, and laid it inside his reach. He picked it up, checked the cylinder, and gave it back.

"I heard you carried an English weapon. Those are harder to come by than this other gear."

I returned it to its scabbard and watched him take the Paterson off cock and put it away. "I heard the Rangers went to Peace-makers."

"Peacemaker didn't save my hide fourteen times in fifty-eight. What's your story?"

That put his age back into the fifties. "I've got a billet at the First Unitarian Church in Owen, where they think I'm a preacher named Sebastian, out of Denver. Governor Ireland asked us to lend a hand with a run of robberies in the panhandle."

"Why Owen?"

"So far it's the only place this bunch

hasn't hit."

"Think it's next?"

"Only if they're foolish enough to tip their hand in their own parlor."

"Just because we carry our guns out in the open don't mean we're simple. We poked our heads into every attic, root cellar, and pigsty in town on the same suggestion. It didn't take long; you'll find out why when you see the place. We didn't turn up a cartwheel dollar unaccounted for nor a man who fit any of the descriptions close enough to sweat a confession out of him."

"Bet you sweated someone, though."

"San Antonio sends out a new Yellow Book every two or three years, to keep us current on who's got paper out on him. Some, when we know where they are, we leave for seed. The seed crop in Owen all had witnesses that put them home at the wrong times. Wrong for us, anyway. I'm satisfied."

"Some of the new breed have never been posted anywhere. They're in it for profit, not to settle old scores. They don't write letters to newspapers or do anything else to bring suspicion to them. You won't find them in your book."

"You want to know the first time I ever heard the words 'new breed'? December sixty-eight, when John Wesley Hardin bush-whacked and killed three Yankee troopers in Sumpter. I been here long enough to see a parcel of new breeds turn old, when they lived that long, and a bushel of new breeds pour in on their heels. You fixing to pray this bunch into turning themselves in?"

"I'm not fixing to do anything but keep my ears open. If the God-fearing folk there tell me something they didn't tell you, I'll report it and you can do what you want with it. We're not after glory."

"Glory, you think that's what this conversation is about?"

I'd pinked him where it hurt. I didn't know why Blackthorne saddled me with these jobs that required diplomacy. The last time I'd had to establish friendly relations with an elite law enforcement unit outside the U.S. marshals, I'd nearly started a war with Canada. "I wasn't born pinned to that star, Captain. I drove cattle between here and Mexico, and someone was always telling thumpers in the bunkhouse. A coroner's jury in San Antonio ruled 'death by suicide' in the case of five bandits mowed down by Texas Rangers because everyone knows what's in store for a desperado who sticks up a bank that close to Rangers headquarters. A reputation like that is worth a

131

thousand extra men. It's in everyone's best interest not to claim outside credit, or glory, if you like that sort of language."

His steel-shot eyes regarded me from under brows that stuck out like spines. The resemblance to the man behind the counter in the train station was marked. He tilted back his chair, scooped the wide framed photograph off its hook with one hand, banged the front legs back down, and laid the picture on my side of the table facing my way. A stone barracks stretched behind the two rows of armed men, with empty sky above and barren earth below. On the bottom, in brown ink in a neat copperplate hand, someone had written:

Ft. Sill, 10 June 1875

"That's me, Sergeant Andrew Jackson Jordan, aged none-of-your-goddamn business." His index finger banged the glass above a face that was all bone and a pair of eyes that photographed like blank whites, belonging to one of the Rangers seated on the ground. He'd worn chin whiskers then and the handlebars were smaller. Apart from that I didn't know how a man could have changed so much in nine years. I put him back down into his forties, and the veteran of 1858 around age eighteen.

"These here are Corporal T. J. McReady and Ranger James Poe. Mac and Jimmy. I never knew Mac's Christian name."

I looked at a young Irish roughneck and an Adam's apple with a head attached, seated on either side of the sergeant. He'd had several years on both.

He read my mind. "They called me Dad. They wasn't walking yet when I joined up."

"I guess there's a Dad in every outfit. Mine had one."

"A splay-footed mulatto name of Tilson took the picture about a week after the Comanches surrendered. It was white of the Yankees to let us sit for it, seeing as how they got the glory after we fought the bastards forty years, including the five we spent doing it alone while they was busy putting down rebels. Mac never had his likeness made before and kept asking when would it be ready. He never seen it. He was assassinated June twelfth. It was done from cover with a shotgun, from behind. We never did find who done it or why. Half his head was gone. His mother had to say good-bye to him through the coffin lid. Twenty-two he was."

"What about Poe?"

"Jimmy got tired of manhunting finally and shot himself behind the counter of a dry-goods store in Dallas. Later that day the city marshal found his wife shot dead in their house. Same caliber gun. They fell out over something and he got all the way to work before what he done caught up with him.

"Burial's free when you served with the Rangers. There's your glory."

"We've all got stories like that," I said. "I meant no disrespect."

He leaned back and rehung the picture, more crookedly than before. "We'll all of us be reunited in dust. I gave up on the other. Maybe I shouldn't talk like that in front of a padre."

"I'm not pretending to be a priest. And I'm not half sure you're wrong."

"We'll just leave that in the room, along with this here." He picked up the letter from Judge Blackthorne and set fire to it with a match from a twist of oilcloth he took from his flap pocket. When it had burned almost down to his fingers he let it fall to the floor and stamped out the flame.

I felt like taking off my hat. I'd missed my funeral.

TEN

"Two banks, the Overland, two trains, all in six months," I said. "Blackthorne said this gang leaves footprints, but he didn't say what they were."

"He always cut you loose this well informed?"

"He encourages independent action, outside his presence. To him that means traveling light on such things as too much preparation, which he says slows the brain and the hand. He's a son of a bitch is what he is."

"How's the pay?"

"I can't spend what I make, but that's only because I haven't had a week off since the last time I was shot."

"Sounds familiar. Why do you stick?"

"For the glory, same as you."

Jordan still had his matches out. He filled a short-barreled pipe from a pouch in his other flap pocket and started it, his cheeks caving in on the draw where the molars had rotted away. His front teeth — the lowers, anyway — were ground down to yellow-oak stumps. If he had uppers the handlebars covered them.

He shook out the match, dropped it on the floor, and pushed the pouch toward me. I shook my head.

"You're overplaying your part," he said. "I read the Bible cover to cover and back. San Antonio recommends it. It don't say a thing against smoking or chewing. The Reverend Wilcoxson up at the First Methodist orders cigars by the case from New Orleans."

"I never got the habit."

He puffed smoke out of the side opposite the pipe, which as long as it was burning he never took out of his mouth. "I got a man who won't cuss and some who say they never touched a drop of the Creature, but when it comes to covering ground fast they'll all dump their coffee before their tobacco. I don't trust a man without a vice I can see or smell or taste. The one he's hiding might get me killed."

"I didn't say I didn't have any vices."

"I forgot to mention women, which can be worse than all the rest put together. I'm near certain it was another woman caused

Jimmy Poe to shoot his wife and then himself."

"I approve of women in general, but I've
been on friendly terms with the Creature
most of my life."

"How friendly?"

"We were living in each other's pockets
for a while. The commitment got to be too
much. These days we just shake hands."

"Same here. It was Mrs. Jordan made me
choose. She's dead, but it don't taste the
same now that I don't have to hide it in the
potato bin." He smoked. "I drink standing
up. We got a nice little watering hole down
the street with a cross draft from the river,
though it's best to put it down fast before it
boils."

"After we talk. Bartenders spill too much."

He scratched his congenitally broken
nose. "How many know about this scheme
apart from you, me, and the Judge?"

"Pretty much the entire territory of Montana, and I have my suspicions about the
Santa Fe Railroad. As I see it I've got three
weeks at the outside before everyone in the
panhandle knows I'm still around and
Brother Bernard never was."

"Who's he?"

"He's me. Sebastian's my other name."

"You had too many as it was. I wouldn't

give it no three weeks. News travels faster by jackrabbit than Western Union."

"When's the next stage leave for Owen?"

"Eight in the morning."

"That's another day gone. We'd better get started. Has any of the gang been identified?"

"Not yet. They wear bandannas over their faces and only one does the talking."

"That describes half the men in your book. What is it about the robberies that ties them all to one bunch?"

"It's not so much the way they go about their business as how they look. Everyone that's ever read about Jesse James knows what to say and where to point his pistol and to get in and out fast; if I had my way I'd bring in every one of them dime novelists in leg irons for teaching folks how to break the law. But even they don't say Jesse and his guerrillas dressed alike even in the war."

"They wear uniforms?"

"Not so's you'd call 'em that, taken one at a time. When five men bust in all wearing white dusters, gray hats, and blue bandannas, that's the impression. That's how it's been all six times."

"Six? I counted five raids."

He plucked the piece he'd cut from the

138

Gazette off his spindle and slapped it down in front of me. It was a sketchy description of a midnight run on a cattle ranch near a town called White Horse three days earlier. The thieves had shot the ranch hand on watch and turned five hundred head of Herefords north. Contact had been made with the Texas Rangers to investigate.

"What makes this our gang?" I asked.

"They gut-shot the man on watch, but he was still talking when the man that came to fetch us took us to the line shack where they carried him. He didn't talk long. There was a little-bitty moon that night, what we call a rustler's moon, but it was enough to see what they was wearing."

"Dusters are common in dusty country. They could've had on brown hats and red bandannas. You can't see colors by moonlight."

"Nor did he, but different colors look different whatever the light. They was all the same. I say they was gray and blue."

"Too thin for court."

"It's a far piece out here between courts. They don't always make it."

"Five men?"

"Seven. I said it was five bust in on banks and such, but I didn't mention the one they left outside with a carbine and the one they left to hold the horses. At White Horse, the other hands had put together a P.C. and took out after them; we met them on their way back. They'd followed to the Canadian, where the bunch turned the herd into the river, but by then the moon was down and they couldn't see where they come out. The hands voted against making camp on account of the bushwhack risk."

"P.C." was Texas talk for *posse comitatus.* Guerrillas had brought the term west from Missouri; in many cases half a jump ahead of a posse. "Did you find where they came out?"

He nodded, puffing smoke. "It was sunup and the trail was cold. In the Nations it crossed some others left by legitimate outfits headed to market. We wired Fort Smith to alert the marshals, but them beeves are gone. Chicago's hungry."

"Where's White Horse?"

"Thirty miles southwest of where you're headed. Your Judge Blackthorne might be on the sunny side of right. Then again he might not."

"He might not. Rustling's hard work for cash bandits. They don't usually cross over."

"If it's the new breed, where'd they learn to ride if not a working ranch? I'm seeing a lot more buggies and buckboards than saddle horses these days."

"I notice you're not ready for a buggy yet. If you rode out there and up into the Nations and back in three days, you ought to be lathered up as bad as your mount."

"That ugly little mustang needs more'n a short trot like that to break a sweat. I wish I could say the same for me. I just got back from the bathhouse when you knocked."

"When do you sleep?"

"When it hits. Some nights I don't make it as far as that cot."

"How many men do you have under you?"

"Fourteen. I came here with a company, but that was before the Frontier Batallion busted up. We done too good a job thinning out rebel scum, you see."

"You should've left a few more for seed."

"Wouldn't of done. Austin discovered Mexico and took all my best men. There's a powerful lot of ranch money down on the border and the governor's fixing to keep it in this country where he can draw on it come election time. That's what this bunch is counting on. It's a wonderment they took this long to test me."

"Why do they dress alike, you figure?"

"Keep from shooting each other."

"How much shooting takes place?"

"Less than you'd expect. They winged the

shotgun messenger on the Overland to make their point, but that was the worst of it till they killed that cowhand on watch. A bank manager got pistol-whipped when he forgot the combination to the safe, if you count that and if you count bankers. I won't say they go out of their way not to let blood, but they don't rattle. If that's the new way of robbing folks, I'm for it, and I'll shake their hands on the scaffold."

"I'd admire to have a talk with that shotgun messenger."

"Not the banker?"

"Him too, but shotgun men have good eyes and remember what they see."

"Just as well. The banker took his busted head home to Baltimore. The shotgun's staying with his sister in Owen till he heals, but I believe they're affiliated with the Church of Rome."

"I'll visit as a neighbor." I took out the sorry wallet and showed him the telegram from R. Freemason, director of the First Unitarian Church. "What can you tell me about him?"

"He ain't Catholic."

"I gathered that from the name."

"Dick Freemason runs sheep, not that you'd smell it on him. He's a gentleman rancher, lives in town with his wife in a big ugly house he had built, with a chandelier he had shipped from Italy and sent a special train down to fetch it. He sits on most of the town committees and had a big hand in banning whores from all the public areas before ten P.M. He pays exactly twice as many men as he needs to manage his spread. Ask me why."

"Because he runs sheep in cattle country."

He tried not to appear impressed. "You're quicker than you look."

"That's why I get these assignments. I suppose you asked his hired guns what they were doing at the time of the robberies."

"I did. I work this job. I'd of been suspicious if they all had stories, and I'm pretty sure at least two of them are in the Yellow Book under other names. But Freemason pays too much to make the risk worthwhile."

"No one pays that much."

"He comes close. Also he's a rough cob under the silk. Eleven jurors voted to send him to Huntsville after he had a bunkhouse thief horsewhipped to death. That was in Waco, before he came here. I don't know where he was before that. He don't talk like a Texan."

He took the pipe out of his mouth then to stifle a yawn. I was keeping him from his cot. I got up. "I'll pass on that drink.

Brother Bernard shouldn't be seen in a saloon in broad daylight. Is there a place in town where I can put up my feet?"

"Corporal Thomson and his wife have a spare room and a baby on the way. They can use the money. White house with green shutters, two squares up and one over. Where's the rest of your gear?"

"I left it with the station agent. He looks enough like you to be kin."

"First cousin. I won't apologize for his manners. He was easier to live with before he hurt his back and had to leave the Rangers."

"Is he the reason you didn't volunteer for the border?"

"It meant promotion to major, but I turned it down when they offered. He can't ride and he can't sit up in a train. Since Elizabeth died the miserable bastard's all the family I got."

I shook his hand. "I'm Sebastian if Corporal Thomson asks."

"I recommend it. She's all right, but he likes to talk."

"Did the jury in Waco ever find out if Freemason wanted that man whipped to death?"

"I never heard."

"Maybe he's easier on the ministers who

work for him."

He yawned openly. "Stick your fingers in the collection plate and find out."

ELEVEN

I never had the opportunity to board the gondola of a hot-air balloon, but I've ridden in Pullman parlor cars, and someone once said that apart from them no nineteenth-century invention accommodated itself to the comfort of passengers as well as the Concord coach: more than a ton of red-lacquered bentwood, suspended hammock fashion on a pair of leather thoroughbraces that rocked its human cargo gently over washes and rubble. But it was wasted on flat west Texas, so I didn't get one.

Wells, Fargo & Company, owner of the Overland, had sent all its Concords to more challenging country and stuck me in a square mud wagon on solid elmwood timbers that telegraphed every ridge and chuck-hole directly to my spine. Dust caked the muslin side curtains, releasing gusts of ocher powder when the cords were undone but forming no barrier whatsoever to fresh injections from outside. When they were drawn and tied down, the hot wind battered at them and whenever we turned crosswise to the blast the coach wobbled and groaned and tried to heel over like a ship. One of my fellow travelers, a barbed-wire salesman from Indiana who carried a sample case that opened in two halves to show his assortment of Buckthorns, Champions, Spur Rowels, and Sawteeth mounted on washboards, offered to bet me that at times we were rolling on two wheels only, the others lifted clear of the earth and spinning ineffectually.

I declined to take him up on the wager. Partly it was because I wasn't half convinced he was wrong, but mostly it was because I was in full preacher's kit, with the Deane-Adams well concealed beneath the rusty black sackcloth of my old coat and a badly used slouch hat that ought to have had a couple of holes cut in the brim for an ass to stick its ears through, and games of chance were inappropriate. I smiled as I shook my head, clinging to the valise on my lap and trying not to cut my throat with Eldred Griffin's stiff clerical collar.

The first time I'd tried it on, in Corporal and Mrs. Thomson's spare bedroom in Wichita Falls, I'd looked at myself in the mirror above the wash basin and saw a mean-faced, middle-aged gunman trying to pass as a man of the cloth, but of course I was hobbled by guilty knowledge. I'd known preachers who could match a Kansas redleg for ruthless aspect and the saintliest-looking one I'd ever seen, with white hands and a gentle countenance, had hanged himself in a cell in Billings after clubbing his wife to death with a boot scraper during a heated discussion over some little thing. I promised myself to shave more closely and look to my nails and accept the rest with serenity.

The collar was another matter. I wasn't sure I'd ever get used to it in the Texas heat and there were plenty of sects that didn't require it, but having been seen with it on, I considered putting it away a risk to my mission. Griffin had outmaneuvered me at the last. The torturous gift was his vengeance for having been forced to compromise his principles. It was my hair shirt.

I kept the valise close because it contained his sermons. I'd given him my word I'd look after them, and I was rewarded for my vigilance when the driver turned abruptly to avoid striking some piece of wagon-road jetsam, overcorrected, and an iron-bound trunk toppled off the rack on the roof, broke its hasp when it struck the ground, and spilled out most of its contents. The driver drew rein and my only other companion, a careworn lawyer who dressed even more shabbily than I did, got out to scoop his linen and legal library back into the trunk. The mustard-colored volumes had been missent to Houston while following him from St. Louis; after they were rerouted by the railroad, he'd left his brand-new practice in Owen to go to Wichita Falls and bring them home personally.

I got that information from his anxious conversation with the driver while the trunk was being loaded, and he repeated it as he repacked. The heat and dust of the journey had not led to casual conversation except from the wire drummer, who seldom heard what was said in answer and failed to draw the obvious conclusion from silence.

The lawyer struck me as a worthier fellow. I respect a man who takes care of the tools of his trade; Blackthorne treated his soiled, mismatched texts as tenderly as a surgeon handles his saws and scalpels, and if I were on trial for my life I'd want no one else to sit in judgment.

Provided I was innocent.

The driver, who cursed the way other men breathed, bound the trunk with rope from the tackle in the boot to keep it from flying open again while his shotgun messenger stood by with the hammers eared back on his Stevens ten-gauge, dividing his attention equally between open country and the tattered attorney. He kept his counsel as to how the man might have rigged the mishap to lay the stage open to ambush. Guarding mail shipments is a suspicious profession.

There was no faulting his caution. There must have been something of value in the strongbox, because the passenger fares on that run wouldn't have fed the horses, much less paid for the wear and tear on the equipment.

The salesman and I stepped down to stretch our legs. It did nothing for my confidence in my disguise that the messenger watched me as closely as he did the others. His taut face and bunched chin beneath the black whiskers was the first evidence I'd seen that the recent bandit raids had the panhandle on the balls of its feet.

I asked the lawyer for his card.

He didn't hear me at first, concentrating as he was on the driver's skill with knots. Then he hoisted his bushy brows and smiled tragically at me from under muttonchops that had needed barbering a week ago. Gray tips and the general fall of his crest made him look ten years older than he probably was. He might have been on the green side of thirty-five.

"I thought you parsons pled your case with the Almighty Imponderable," he said. "I'm afraid I'm not licensed to practice before that bench."

I answered the smile with a humble one of my own, or rather of Brother Bernard's. "I've no use for fence, but I took that gentleman's name." I tilted my head toward the third member of our party, who was relieving himself noisily into a clump of thorn scrub at the side of the road. I'd already forgotten what he called himself. "I see no reason not to make a running jump at getting to know my neighbors. Bernard Sebastian." I offered my hand.

"Father or Reverend?" He took it, stealing a look at my raiment. The treasures of the Vatican were not apparent.

"Brother. I'm merely a pilgrim on the path to righteousness."

"Well, Brother, you must have been walking it on your hands. I've shaken the paws of mule skinners with less muscle." He kneaded bruised fingers.

I apologized, stopping short of inventing an excuse. I would have to watch more than just my visual impression. The strength in my gun hand ill befit the meek.

He seemed to disregard it. "I haven't just had time to have cards printed. I've spent my first weeks in Texas tracking that trunk, which has scaled mountains and forded rivers and crossed the burning prairie, passing all manner of savages and baggage clerks, only to become a casualty twenty-five miles from its destination."

The driver hooked a heel on a corner of the item under discussion and heaved back on the rope to set the knot. "Better a busted trunk than a busted wheel. The Golden Rule don't hold up out here."

"You're hardly the resident expert," said the lawyer. To me: "I'm Luther Cherry. I expect delivery of my shingle any time, if that dullard of a sign painter ever gets it right. Why a man who can't spell should choose that line of work is a question only your immortal Client can answer."

"I'm sure He can, although I'd hesitate to approach Him with it. What kind of law do you practice?"

"Real property, chiefly land disputes; which makes me a colleague of sorts of Mr. Barbed Wire. I'd intended to open an office in Denver, but there's a glut there, as you might expect. Then I learned the legislature in Austin is debating a law to declare fence-cutting a felony. In Colorado Territory it's a misdemeanor punished by a fine, which Big Cattle pays routinely as part of the cost of running off their smaller competitors' stock."

"They'll never pass it," I said. "It would mean the end of the open range in this state."

"Cattle don't pay taxes. Landowners do, and entirely too much of it is going to waste on community grazing rights. In any case I anticipate a healthy demand for my counsel."

"I'm told ranchers here are accustomed to settling their disputes out in the open, with gunfire."

"I was told the same thing, and most of the inquiries I made confirmed it, when they received a response at all. The guard is changing, however, as change it must, before the relentless advance of civilization. The governor is in favor of the law, and he has the support of Mr. Richard Freemason of Owen, who wired me travel expenses in St. Louis as part of the retainer for my services."

The sheep baron seemed to cast a wide loop.

"We share a sponsor," I said. "Mr. Freemason is a director of the church where I am preparing to preach the gospel."

Some of the tragedy went out of Cherry's smile. "A splendid sign! The sheep wars have been strangling the livestock industry, and Mr. Freemason means to have a hand in restoring peace. Was not the man whose wife bore the Prince of Peace a shepherd?"

"This one, at least, has made friends of two strangers."

"Will a Mrs. Sebastian be joining you later, or does your oath forbid the domestic custom?"

"It doesn't, but I have no wife."

His face fell. "That's a disappointment. Mrs. Cherry is closing the house in St. Louis and will board with her parents until I'm settled. It's lonely out here for a woman, they say."

"Mr. Freemason is married."

"I've not met him yet, though I've spoken with his wife, who told me he was away visiting the ranch until this week. She's gracious, but worldly — a bit out of Anna's set. She paints her face. The only other women I've seen are years older, except the ones who can't show themselves until the respectable citizens are home in bed." Abruptly he added, "Those who are not engaged until late setting their office in order, I mean."

154

He'd colored a shade, surprising me. None of the lawyers I'd known could have managed it.

"Yes," I said, acknowledging the problem of Original Sin. "Still, it's not exactly a mining camp."

"Did I hear you say you're bound for the camps?" The fence man joined us, buttoning his fly. He picked up only half of everything said within his earshot and folded it into a pitch. "Once I make my stake in Texas I'm off to the gold-fields. There's nothing like six hundred yards of Glidden's Twist Oval to protect your claim from jumpers."

Cherry shook his head — not to contradict the other's impression of what we were talking about, but to address the new development. He'd do well in court. "I studied the crime for my bar examination. Claims are jumped in town, not in the field. It's a combination of bookkeeping and bribery."

The salesman considered what he'd taken from that, then lost interest. "They ain't come up with a barb for that yet." He climbed back aboard the coach.

The driver manhandled the trunk to the roof and lashed it to the rack. His messenger waited until we were all seated, then eased down his hammers and mounted to his place on top. As we jolted forward, Cherry

155

watched the flat land rolling past. "It's this way clear to Owen. Does it ever change, do you think?"

I said, "I understand after you cross the Canadian it starts to level out."

He turned from his window, but I was careful not to intercept his look. The man sitting facing us was busy rearranging the samples in his case. I hoped — well, prayed — that if I learned to think before I spoke I might play my part as well as they played theirs.

TWELVE

Owen, Texas, was ten years old, older than Wichita Falls by five years and ancient by frontier standards, which had seen pick holes sprout into metropolises in six months, then blow away six weeks after the veins played out, and roaring end-of-track towns dismantle themselves and reassemble under different names farther down the ever-expanding line. Such places were as transient as Indian villages and left only piles of offal behind to mark their passage. Owen had kept the offal but refused to budge.

Increase Owen, scion of an old New England family and a putative former army major who had either resigned or been cashiered by Ranald MacKenzie at the end of the Red River Indian War in 1874, had built an adobe store on a tributary of the Canadian River called Wild Horse Creek, selling whiskey and provisions and ammunition to parties of buffalo hunters. On occasion he'd bartered for hides, and at the end of the first winter — and they were as cold in the panhandle as the summers were unbearably hot — when the stack of stiff green hides behind the building began to reek, he sold them to a tanner, who paid the market rate. This amounted to ten times what he'd taken in on all his other merchandise since opening his doors, wiping out cost of construction and stock. At that point he entered into a partnership with the tanner. With the Eastern demand for lap robes and doctors' coats and leather belts to drive the gears in Industrial Age manufactories at its peak, he might have retired in five years to a life of leisure and fine things if the buffalo had just held out.

They didn't. By then a little community had sprung up around the store, made up of gunsmiths, knife sharpeners, wheelwrights, crib girls, faro dealers, plank-bar saloons where busthead whiskey was sold and consumed by the jug, and all the other bluebottles that feed on a going concern. Owen had had the foresight to obtain a deed to a hundred acres on the creek and the knowledge to have it platted for town lots, but also the poor judgment to do it all on credit. When the great herds vanished and his debtors caught up with him, he shot himself with the Army Colt he'd carried in the Battle of Palo Duro Canyon; or had stolen from a sutler's after he'd been stripped of his weapons and rank, depending upon which story you preferred. Generally there's truth in everything that's said about a person, and if you took all the rogues out of the rotation the country would still belong to the Indians, who had rogues in plenty but not enough to check the press from the Atlantic coast.

Its founder's misfortune and death would have been the end of the city of Owen in the normal course of things, but the West was no normal place. The creek, which slowed to a trickle during droughts, never quite dried up, and the grazing was ideal for fattening herds of longhorns and Herefords being driven from the ranches down south to the Kansas railheads in Dodge City and Abilene. Tent saloons popped up like mushrooms, to be replaced quickly by frame buildings where brand whiskey was served in bottles on proper bars and brothels with parlors replaced the cribs. There were shootings, brawls, and the odd mysterious disappearance of a lucky poker player after he left the scene of his success, but nothing to compare with what was going on up north, where the cowhands were paid their full trail wages and had more to spend. Owen boasted the first hotel in the panhandle, and soon a Catholic church, attended mainly by Mexican masons and carpenters and their families. In 1878, a sheep rancher named Vallejo wedded the eldest daughter of one of them before its altar and was buried from there three months later after he was shot by an unknown assassin and his flock scattered. No one was ever brought to trial for his murder; just as well, as it was commonly accepted that no Texas jury would find against the cattle interests, which benefited most from discouraging the sheep trade in that state.

That was the beginning of Owen's ranching phase. By the time I arrived, relations between cattleman and shepherd had settled into a low simmer. Residents credited the uneasy truce to the appearance of Richard Freemason, whose eight-hundred-acre ranch on the other side of Wild Horse Creek was the largest in the region, and whose determination to raise sheep placed him on the side of one of the most oppressed groups on the prairie. He was the first rancher to encircle his spread with barbed wire. Three of his fence riders (who when questioned on the stand revealed a deeper knowledge of gun handling than posthole digging) were tried for the murder of a cowhand surprised in the act of cutting the wire to drive some strays across the spread instead of riding a mile out of his way to use the public gate, and convicted after forty minutes of jury deliberation. Freemason appealed the decision. It was upheld and the three were condemned to hang until Governor Ireland issued a full pardon, citing the right of a property owner and his trusties to defend it from trespassers and vandals. He made special note of the relative proximity of the gate and the minor nature of the inconvenience to the cowhand of obeying the law.

The precedent sent shockwaves from the Canadian to the Rio Grande. Prominent supporters of the cattle trade pronounced it a license to commit murder, but since that had been the effect of earlier decisions on the side of Big Cattle, few paid them any attention. Anyone who didn't believe the tide was changing took a ruder hit a few months later when a bill was introduced in the capital to make fence cutting a crime punishable by jail and a stiff fine. Freemason's single-minded crusade on his men's behalf was considered instrumental in this development, and as one public servant after another came forward in favor of the bill, it seemed likely to pass.

I got part of this history from the attendant who took my money and handed me a towel at the bathhouse and the rest from the clerk in the freight office, who took my valise for safekeeping and gave me a ticket to reclaim it. There is something about a clerical collar that brings out the tour guide in everyone. I was clean and close-shaven, but unbrushed. I'd played the impoverished preacher over whether to order the extra service at the launderer's where the bathhouse man had offered to take my clothes while I was soaking, then decided I'd make a better impression in a clean shirt and a white collar and a dusty suit than I would in a brushed one and yellow linen; for I'd chosen to pay a call upon my benefactor as soon as I was presentable. When the collar came back, the helpful launderer had put in enough starch to slice cheese with it.

Finding the house required no directions, although the clerk and the attendant, both proud citizens, had been eager to point it out. It stood on the only high ground in town, a conical hill erected with spades and dredges from level plain that brought the gables in line with the steeple of the Catholic church at the opposite end of the main street. The construction was a delirious arrangement of spires, grilles, turrets, and fretwork, with fishscale shingles and more shades of paint than a tart caught outside in daylight. A quartet of mature cottonwoods provided shade on all four sides at what must have been considerable expense; trees don't grow in such accommodating symmetry and so had to have been brought in after the house was built.

On my way there I passed the First Unitarian church, a much simpler affair of whitewashed wood with a squat bell tower, common unstained windows, and its name painted in block letters on the lintel above the door. A squat woman with her hair in a bun quit sweeping the front steps to watch me pass in my working uniform. When I touched my hat, she stopped leaning on her broom and got back to business.

A long flight of steps cut from native limestone and sunk into the hill led to the front porch of the house. The porch was semicircular, with fluted Greek columns supporting a gothic roof and a shark's-mouth transom above the front door in the Queen Anne style. It was a crazy sort of house until you realized its architect had sought the effect of an ancient English castle that had acquired new additions in many styles over hundreds of years. Then you remembered you were in Texas and it went back to being a crazy sort of house.

The compass-and-square symbol of the Ancient and Honorable Fraternity of Free and Accepted Masons was carved in the center of the paneled mahogany door. I found a blue china bell pull and used it. The ringing on the other side was barely audible. Whoever had constructed the walls and door had built them to withstand a battering ram.

A fine-boned Mexican of around seventy, small as a boy, with white hair and dressed in a loose white cotton shirt and trousers, opened the door. His feet were brown and bare in woven-leather sandals and his face was the color of dark honey and every bit as smooth. Mine had more wrinkles.

I took off my hat and gave him Sebastian's name. "I think Mr. Freemason is expecting me."

"Please come in." No accent accompanied the words.

He closed the door behind me, took my hat, and left me standing in a baronial foyer with a fourteen-foot ceiling, wainscoted with polished walnut six feet up, and furnished on either side with a bench and a chair with high straight backs that looked as inviting as iron maidens. The windows were equipped with wooden shutters that could be swung shut and bolted from inside, with gun ports that would assume the shape of the Swiss cross when the shutters were closed. Either the owner of the house was a fiend on the subject of security or he'd come prudently prepared to defend himself during sheep wars.

In a little while the old man returned, his sandals making no sound at all on the parquet floor, and led me past a cantilevered staircase and down a hall hung with English hunting prints to another paneled door and swung it wide. He held it while I went through the opening and pressed it shut behind me with a faint gasp of a click. The room was an office large enough to contain two of Texas Rangers Captain Jordan's and the post office next door. There were panels on the walls, dark and ancient, a row of oaken file cabinets, several tables scattered with newspapers and Eastern periodicals, and a gargantuan desk six feet tall that opened out into rows of compartments and drawers for letters, stationery, rolls of paper, and ledgers, with a hinged writing surface and scrolled architectural features that probably doubled as secret niches revealed

165

only by hidden mechanisms known only to the cabinetmaker and the owner. When closed, the fixture would assume the appearance of a chifforobe built to shelter a foppish collection of gentlemen's suits of clothes. It was made of cherrywood, deep red and glistening, with burled-walnut insets; an office in itself, redundantly contained within an office.

It impressed me more than anything else I'd seen since I'd spotted the house on my way into town. This marvel of nineteenth-century business machinery was only the third one I'd seen; the others had stood in the private office of the president of the biggest bank in Louisiana and a brokerage firm in Chicago, and they had not been as ornate, the median model geared for less extravagant budgets. I'd heard J. Pierpont Morgan had one in his New York City mansion, but this was my first personal experience of one in a private house.

The man seated in front of it, in a padded leather chair swiveled to face me, was somewhat less impressive physically, but then the dimensions of the house and his reputation had prepared me for a large man on the order of Grover Cleveland or Jumbo the elephant; one of those notorious trenchermen who ate a bucket of oysters for breakfast, sides of pork for dinner, and blew their noses into silk handkerchiefs the size of bedsheets. Richard Freemason was not a small man in comparison to his Mexican manservant, but compact, with slender hands adorned only with a Masonic ingot on the left little finger and a narrow torso in a snug waistcoat of figured silk, small feet in calfskin shoes that gleamed like polished mahogany, and a sandy Vandyke beard trimmed by a barber who ought to have been making violins or miniature portraits in enamel. The only thing large about him was his forehead, which bulged out from the bridge of his nose like Lawrence Lazarus Little's, but with a lower hairline and a sharp widow's peak that made him appear more lupine than leonine. A dedicated phrenologist would have coveted that head, shaved and pickled and marked out in ink like a butcher's chart, the choice cuts labeled Reason, Aggression, Strategy, and Logic. Humor and Fear would occupy the tiniest compartments, like the ones reserved for wire brads in the Brobdingnagian desk.

Tightly packaged men are restrained as a rule, preferring to let the other fellow make the first gesture. Richard Freemason appeared to exist outside the rules. The moment the door snicked shut, he sprang from the chair and strode the distance between us in half the time of a long-legged man, seizing my hand in a grip that was not so much ironclad as electric; when we broke contact, I still felt the tingle to my fingertips.

"Damned glad to see you!" His tenor voice was clipped, telegraphic, with a British edge that might have been affected, but was too narrow to expose as outright fraud. "I hope you'll pardon the blasphemy, but between the kneelers and the Scotchmen and the poured-in-the-mold Dutch Reformed I've been on the defensive longer than the Jews. Do you know the Baptists say that both my blessed parents and nine-tenths of the world are in hell merely because they didn't embrace Christ as their savior? Surely the devil's ship is sunk to the gunnels."

It was the most succinct description of the Catholic, Presbyterian, and Calvinist faiths I'd heard, including Eldred Griffin's. The Baptists always summed up quickly.

"All paths lead to God," was all I could think of to say.

"A most Christian sentiment."

"Actually it's Buddhist. I studied the world's religions for purposes of comparison." Which was true of Eldred Griffin, whose apostasy had sent him in various directions searching for a substitute.

The sheepman didn't seem to disregard this statement so much as file it away for future review. Unlike Judge Blackthorne, he would be a difficult man to annoy. He waved me into a Morris chair in a reading corner beside a barrister case lined with sets bound in morocco and returned to his swivel. I noticed his back never touched the back of the chair. "How was your journey from Denver?"

"Educational. This is the farthest I've ever been from home. I was engaged for many years caring for my poor mother."

"Have you lived in Colorado Territory your entire life?"

I allowed myself — him, too — a small smile. "Only until eight years ago, when it became a state."

"That was clumsy of me. You must understand I have enemies who think they can benefit by surrounding me with spies. May I ask for some documentation? Costumes are easily come by."

"Certainly." I drew out the shabby wallet and gave him the telegram I'd received from him by way of Denver. He glanced at it and returned it. I had the impression he was inventorying the rest of the wallet's contents as I slid the flimsy back inside.

"Your predecessor, the Reverend Rose, retired last month to live with his daughter and son-in-law in California. He was a holy man but a trial at the pulpit, and the lay fellows who have been filling in read directly from the Bible. If you can manage not to put half the congregation to sleep, you'll be a success."

"I haven't had much practice in public, but I've come with a collection of original sermons."

"Did you write them yourself?"

"I dictated them to an acquaintance. I think best while pacing." It was plagiarism, but any reference to my mentor might inspire questions whose answers wouldn't hold up to scrutiny. If he got hold of Griffin's sermons and compared the writing to mine, the differences would be explained.

"I think you'll find the accommodations behind the church comfortable. Sunday is the day after tomorrow. Do you think you'll be settled enough to preside?"

"I'm looking forward to it."

The door opened and a woman leaned in. She hesitated when she saw me. The look she gave me was long and cool. "I'm sorry, Richard. I thought you were alone."

I gripped the arms of my chair hard enough to leave nail marks in the leather and rose behind my host.

"Quite all right, dear. I wanted you to meet Brother Bernard Sebastian, our new minister. My wife."

She closed the door and rustled her skirts across the floor to offer her hand. It was as cool as her eyes, which were blue in the porcelain pallor of her face. She was some years younger than her husband. "Welcome to Owen, sir." Her voice was a contralto, sandy at the edges, thrilling. Before I could thank her she turned toward Freemason. "You asked me to remind you of your committee meeting."

"Is it so late?" He confirmed the time by a gold watch no thicker than a coin and returned it to his waistcoat. "Please forgive me, Brother. Some scoundrel wants to build a saloon on the site we've set aside for a school, and there are one or two fools on the committee whose priorities are suspect." As he spoke he removed a Prince Albert lined in white silk from a hall tree and shrugged into it.

"I'll pray you triumph," I managed to say.

"Dear, the brother has come many miles, the last several in that torture trap of a stage from Wichita Falls. Please offer him refreshment."

"Of course."

He grasped my hand again and left. Mrs. Freemason swung her gaze back to me. "He means tea."

"I was afraid of that."

She wore a pale green satin dress with a square neckline that exposed her collarbone, a fine one that shone like polished marble. She unclasped a thin gold chain from around her neck with the air of one undressing and used the tiny key attached to unlock a cabinet behind a wall panel. "Fielo is a wonderful servant, but he has a problem. Richard carries his key on his watch chain." From the recess she drew a bottle of Hermitage and two cut-crystal glasses, which she filled to the rims on the writing surface of the great desk.

"You won't get anywhere with that dog collar, Page." She handed me a glass. "The devil isn't a fool."

THIRTEEN

I smiled, ill feeling it. "How long has it been, Colleen? Three years. It was Mrs. Baronet then. You were in widow's weeds."

"I was Mrs. Bower again when I met Richard, but don't take any courage from that. You've nothing to gain from threatening to expose me. I told him my story."

"Even Poker Annie?"

"Especially Poker Annie. Other names I went by, too, that even you don't know. He'd have found out about all of them in time. Many people owe him favors. One of them is letting them live. But you're aware of that."

"I heard about the horse whipping in Waco."

She made a face, not that it lessened her attraction. Her hair was still startlingly black, without assistance, and when she wore it piled on her head as today she looked like a Spanish princess painted by a

Renaissance artist who wanted to keep his job. Except for the blue eyes, of course. They were as Irish as her name. Luther Cherry, the lawyer, had said she painted her face, but he must've been sensitive about such things. She knew how to apply it so that it called attention to her best features rather than to itself.

"Richard put a fool in charge and nearly paid for his poor judgment with his life," she said. "It was ironic that the one thing that tripped him up was someone else's fault."

I pretended disinterest. She obviously thought I'd come to spy on Freemason, as he'd suspected himself, and setting her straight wouldn't teach me anything about my supposed employer, who'd begun to interest me. We were seated, I in the Morris chair, she in her husband's business throne before the desk. She filled it better. She was slender, but her skirts and petticoats just fit between the arms and although she wasn't tall, the way she held herself, with her back straight and her chin lifted, gave that impression. Her narrow feet were encased in green satin slippers that matched the dress, her trim ankles in black stockings.

I'd seen her without all those things, or anything else, and she had been just as much of a pleasure to look at, treacherous as she was. Colleen Bower and I went back five years and a thousand miles.

I took a drink and sighed. Hermitage is good sipping whiskey, and I'd been dry since the day of my untimely death. "I suppose it'd be a waste of time to try to convince you I've put aside my wicked past to carry the Word to the heathen."

"Why not as Brother Page? Bernard Sebastian is just the kind of name Harlan Blackthorne would invent. How is the old bastard; ailing, I trust? I heard his heart was stricken, but I didn't credit it. He hasn't one."

"It didn't mellow him. Can a man who's heard the Call not change his name and wipe the slate?"

"I read newspapers. I confess I felt a twinge of regret when I read of your assassination."

I gave it up as a bad investment. She'd been a professional cardsharp for years and was impossible to bluff. "That was the Judge's idea, too, in case someone recognized me. People believe what they read in print, God knows why." I felt my face twisting at the blasphemy. The clothes had begun to wear the wearer.

"I won't, from now on. This is about what

happened in Montana Territory, isn't it? That ogre in Helena never forgets a slight."

"It was a little more than a slight." I said it without thought, not wanting to hesitate and tip my hand. I'd been sure from the start Judge Blackthorne hadn't sent me to Texas as a favor to Austin.

"An injury, then; and to his reputation, which is the only place he can be stung. What's the statute of limitations on a wound to a man's pride?"

"None, where he's concerned. I wasn't aware you'd met." I was still trying to draw her out.

"We haven't. But friends of mine have, and they came to regret it. That was neither here nor there to me until just now, when I found out he still has his sights set on Richard."

"I'd forgotten you're always loyal to your husbands."

She drew healthily from her glass and set it on the desk. She looked thoughtful; but then her expressions operated independently of her honest emotions, if indeed anything about her was honest. "Like Judge, like deputy, I see," she said. You're still holding me responsible for what happened in San Sábado."

"Breen, too. Don't forget Breen."

"Everyone else has. The place doesn't even exist anymore. In the meantime I've heard rumors about your time in Canada and San Francisco. You're growing notorious."

"You do read newspapers."

"Not only that. You've become a staple of the ten-cent press. I can't wait to see what they'll write about your time in Owen."

The Man Who Died Twice," I said, "if this conversation is allowed to leave this room."

"At long last you've learned fear. Are you begging for my silence?"

"I'm asking for it. It won't have to be for long, just until I've finished what I haven't started yet."

"I cannot believe you expect me to conspire in a plot against my husband."

There was nothing for it. There never had been, but I'd been bound to make the attempt. "I'm not here for Freemason, whatever he's done. I never came across his name until I read it in a telegram to Brother Bernard on my way here. He sent it himself, inviting me to replace the Reverend Rose, whoever he may have been."

"You always were an accomplished liar. I'm glad we never played poker in earnest."

"I give you my word if the job has anything to do with Freemason I wasn't told."

"Then what is the job?"

"I won't tell you that."

She nodded. "At least you didn't say you can't. That's one lie even you couldn't bring off."

The subject needed changing. It wasn't as if we'd forget to come back to it. "How did you hook up with Freemason?"

"In Waco. I was dealing faro in a place called the Hispaniola, in a district known as the Reservation, where vice was licensed and taxed. The owner had an arrangement with the local collector, but he neglected to tell me. Five minutes after the dirty little man tapped out, I was in jail on some trumped-up ordinance prohibiting women from playing games of chance in the public room. Richard saw the arrest, figured out what had happened, and had me out on bail in a half hour; it was Friday night, and otherwise I'd have been stuck in that cell until the arraignment Monday morning. Somehow my court date never was set. That was before the infamous horse whipping, which gave his enemies in the cattle trade an opportunity to remove him as an inconvenience. By then we were married."

"He wouldn't accept a simple thank you?"

She picked up her glass and drank. "I'd throw this in your face if it didn't mean I'd have to pour another. I don't want to give him the impression I share Fielo's problem. Naturally I can't tell him I joined his new minister in a drinking bout."

"Does that mean you won't peach?"

" 'Peach.' You did visit San Francisco." She rattled her nails on the glass. She used a clear polish or else one of palest coral; Colleen was not self-effacing, but nor was she vulgar. "I've been sitting here thinking I'd be foolish not to keep you where I can watch you for the time being. Next time, Blackthorne might send someone I won't be able to spot so easily."

"I'll take that with thanks."

"I'm not doing it for you. If it comes down to you or Richard — well, you cannot make me believe you ever expected to die in bed."

"What happened in Montana Territory?"

"Why are you in Texas?"

We'd come around in a circle. She knew now that by mentioning the place at all she'd given me more information than I'd come with, but the only victory I could take from that was partial acceptance of my pledge that Freemason wasn't my target. She'd be dealing no more lucky hands.

I cradled my drink in my palms. "What do you do all day, besides make sure Fielo stays out of the liquor?"

"I keep the books for the ranch, sign the draughts for payroll and expenditures, threaten suppliers with legal action when they short us. With what's left I maintain the household accounts. It's not that much different from operating a card concession."

"This house alone would be more challenging. I heard about the chandelier from Italy."

"Venice," she said. "We hung it in the upstairs ballroom. Actually it sat in a crate on a dock in New Orleans for fourteen months before Richard bought it from a cotton merchant in St. Louis for less than the cost of shipping. The man managed to go broke while it was crossing the Atlantic. Everything in this house was acquired for a fraction of its value, including the building materials, scavenged from the failure of others, and we've borrowed against all of it, every penny. I'll bet you the price of this hideous desk you have more cash available than Richard and I."

"I wouldn't know what to do with the desk. All the paperwork I've ever done would be lost in the top row of pigeonholes. What keeps you from going under with the others?"

"The future of the sheep market. Sheep are cheaper to graze than cattle, because they don't have to be fat to produce wool, and the wool is less expensive to ship. We invest little in breeding, because the same flock continues to produce without replacement; shearing isn't fatal, like skinning and butchering. When we've gotten all the coats and mufflers and mittens we can from a ewe or a ram, we sell it for the hide and meat. Anyone with half a head for figures can see there's less maintenance and more profit in sheep. I'm not saying the cattle will go the way of the buffalo, but in a generation the worst enemies of the trade will have to run sheep just to subsidize the cost of maintaining a meat herd. Richard's associates know that, and are willing to let their investments ride for a few years until the sheep wars come to an end. You've heard what's happening in Austin?"

"I heard he had a hand in it. How many more gunmen will he have to snatch from the gallows before you're in the black?"

She leaned forward slightly in her seat, a maneuver I remembered from sitting across a table from her. It was a rare male player who could divide his concentration between the shadows inside her bodice and the suits he was holding. "We've begun to hear the same argument from the beef barons," she said. "In nearly the same words sheepmen used back when the horse was in the other stall. It's a cry for mercy. By now you've read enough of the Old Testament to know the traditional answer to that."

"I didn't know *you'd* read it."

"My father was a choirmaster. I won't tell you where or with which church; I play close and don't allow anyone to stand behind me. He expected his children to be theosophical prodigies — encouraged it with the flat of his belt, and sometimes the buckle. You've seen the scars."

I had. I'd thought it ungentlemanly to inquire.

"God entered into a wager with Satan that His most faithful servant could not be shaken from his faith. It cost Job everything: property, wife, children, sanity. He cried, 'Why has Thou forsaken me?' God could not answer because of the terms of the bet. Even then, Job refused to forsake God, Who once He'd collected His winnings rewarded his loyalty with property, a new wife, and a litter of children to replace what he'd lost. He thought by that stroke to have compensated Job in full for his dead wife and slain children, incidentally ignoring what *they'd* lost. The story had a great influence on me. When I ran away from home I pledged always to be the one who placed the bet, not the one who was bet upon." She sat back smiling. "That's why I'm with Richard. In Waco I saw his wager and raised him me."

"It's not a bet in the Bible," I said. "There wasn't a pot for God to scoop into His hat."

"Ask Job's wife and children if there's a distinction."

I shook my head and put aside my glass. "I'm an evangelical. My message is one of redemption and forgiveness."

"That's the New Testament. First came the slaughter."

Fourteen

She asked me when I was taking up my duties.

"Right away, provided you give me a recommendation."

"It's a partnership, not a matriarchy. That system always fails. I've promised you my silence and given you my conditions. I've no reservations about your ability. I've seen you turn a lynch mob into a hospitality committee without even drawing your pistol. Are you wearing it, by the way? There must be a reason for that dreadful sack you have on."

"I left it in my valise at the freight office. I didn't seem to need it to get past a seventy-year-old Mexican."

"You thought you'd be searched."

"The man went to the trouble and expense of constructing a hill so he could look down and see who's coming. I spotted that even before I found out the place was built like a fort. An ordinary preacher might be able to explain why he was armed. I can't afford it."

"That won't always be the case, will it?"

"I didn't bring it all this way to leave it with Wells, Fargo."

"Richard took precautions that were wise when he built the house. Once that fence-cutting bill becomes law, I'll have the shutters taken down and plant roses. There won't be any invading armies to use them for cover."

"In your place I'd wait until someone cuts a fence and see what happens. There's a new lawyer in town with a trunk full of laws and less than half of them with teeth."

She lifted her brows; she didn't pluck them close and they made strong apostrophes above her already expressive eyes. "You've met young Mr. Cherry. You don't waste time."

"I haven't it to waste."

"He doesn't approve of me, but then he's his wife's creature. She's one of those mouse-faced tyrants men wear in lockets around their necks in place of a leash."

"We met on the stage from Wichita Falls, where he went to retrieve his trunk. He didn't show me a likeness."

"Nor me. I spotted it, from as far away as

you spotted this house. Depend upon it, he wears one, and he wouldn't part with it any more than a broke horse would stray far from a loose bridle. I expect that in a horse but I despise it in a man."

"I always wondered what attracted you to me."

"You're too arrogant for the ministry, Page, but that will change. You just haven't met a woman who will stay as long as it takes." Her lips twitched at the corners; her Irish puck was up. "Thank you for the advice about the law. With whose welfare are you concerned, Richard's or mine?"

I picked up my drink and finished it. "He has good taste in whiskey, and the panhandle's ugly enough even with you around for distraction. If something happened to you both I couldn't stand the place."

"It has its virtues. When you find the time to spare you must ride out to Palo Duro Canyon and spend the day. Such country is the real reason Adam left Eden."

"Your father had more influence than you think. You know Scripture better than I do, and I've had a steady diet of it for three weeks."

"I had it for sixteen years. I've had opportunity to go back to the table. Someday you must ask me about Memphis."

"I will," I said. "When I find the time."

She emptied her glass and said nothing, which I interpreted as a dismissal. I stood. "Freemason says I'll be comfortable behind the church. Does that mean no snakes?"

"Mrs. McIlvaine won't have them. She wouldn't have *me* if I weren't Richard's choice. Women don't approve of me any more than house-trained men. They see in me what they gave up when they set out to train them."

"I think we almost met." I described the woman I'd seen sweeping the church steps.

"I don't suppose she was cordial. She saves the energy she might spend on the social graces to assault the dust in the church and parsonage. She seems to tolerate it outdoors, but only because she's life-size and Texas is so big. Texas avoids direct confrontation, however. You'll find less sand in your sheets than anywhere else this side of the gulf."

I turned the glass knob on the door but didn't pull on it. "You said Freemason knows everything about you. What does he know about me? I don't mean Brother Bernard. If he suspected who I was, he wouldn't have left me alone in the house with you."

"He knows I'm no tame blossom." From her loose right sleeve she drew a trim

American Arms pistol hardly bigger than my thumb, then slid it back. It was secured by a rubberized strap to her wrist; a quick flick would have placed it in her palm ready to fire. It's not a comfortable thing to carry around the house, so I guessed she'd taken it from the cabinet with the whiskey. "As for my past, I didn't bore him with details," she said. "I look forward to hearing your sermon Sunday."

"I'll select it with you in mind."

"No Magdalens or Jezebels, I hope. I've always given you credit for being an original thinker."

In the hallway, the old Mexican appeared from the woodwork with my hat and led me to the door. A bolt shot behind me.

I went from there to the freight office for my valise. The friendly clerk asked what I'd thought of the Freemason mansion, as he called it.

"I found it grand, but I'm a man of simple tastes."

"Did you meet Mrs. Freemason?"

"She was quite gracious."

"The wife thinks she's stuck up. I say she's shy. A lot of folks who don't talk much in society are just nervous about saying the wrong thing."

"That's a very Christian thing to say."

He beamed, as if he'd just been baptized. He had a face designed for beaming, red and round between black side-whiskers. He didn't seem eager for me to leave, so I took a chance and asked about the shotgun messenger who'd been shot trying to guard a stage from bandits.

"That's Sweeney," he said. "Charlie Sweet, and he's right named. They all take the work seriously, but I don't think I ever saw him without a smile on his face. He was smiling when they pulled out the slug, I heard. He's helping out in his sister's restaurant, dishing out soup and washing crockery, till he can sit a coach, on account of his back. The Pan Handle, she calls it: two words."

"A clever woman. I thought I might be able to bring him cheer, but from what you say it may be the reverse."

"He'd welcome a visit just the same. He and Jane are papists, but I don't suppose she'd object to Charlie sitting down with any man of the cloth. Between you and me, she works him like a horse. It's a chore to call her Miss Sweet, so most of us just tip our hats or take them off when we visit her establishment, not that it improves her disposition. Good biscuits," he added.

"I'll look in on them first chance I get." I

offered him a nickel for looking after the bag, but he shook his head and smiled.

The door to the First Unitarian church was unlocked. I went inside. The place was clean and unremarkable, with a flight of open steps to the bell tower, bare planks between two rows of polished-pine pews, and a plain pulpit on a platform with two steps leading up to it. A parlor stove was placed just where it needed to be to dry out the coats and hats that would hang from a row of pegs when it rained or snowed; apart from that it was out of place in that simple room, with filigree and mica through which the flame would glow whenever the mercury dipped below broiling. It stood on three elegantly curved legs like a Chippendale chest.

"It was a gift from Mr. Freemason. A common barrel stove would've heated the place just as well."

It was a woman's voice barely, deeper even than Colleen Freemason's, with a burr that might have been smuggled from Scotland and kept in storage to preserve it until that moment. She'd come in through a door that opened onto the raised platform and stood holding her broom bristles up, like a rake. All these many years later, Mrs. McIlvaine remains one of my strongest memories of

Owen, although we never exchanged more than a hundred words in all. I still see her with that broom. I never saw her without it.

She took me through that side door and across a patch of burned-out grass behind the church to a saltbox that stood on the same lot, an afterthought assembled from lumber left over after the church was finished and generously referred to as the parsonage. The sitting room held a rocking chair, a straightback with a caned seat that rocked more predictably on its short leg, and a small laundry stove that could warm a bowl of soup or brew a pot of coffee but not both at the same time, in a space about the size of Eldred Griffin's grim study in the caretaker's shack in Helena. A single partition separated it decently from the pastor's sleeping quarters, where I could lie on the iron-framed bed with a pencil in each hand and write my name on both opposing walls. In ugly weather a white enamel chamber pot under the bed spared the necessity to visit the gaunt little outhouse in the corner of the lot.

The place was spotless, and no wonder. There was little in it to impede the progress of Mrs. McIlvaine's ruthless broom. The Reverend Rose, it developed, had taken his small personal library with him when he went west, leaving me with nothing to occupy my time that first night except the Bible and a brown page of advertising from a newspaper of unknown vintage someone had used to line the drawer in the spavined nightstand. When I tired of the Book of books I learned that at some point in history, gentlemen's English worsted suits of clothes had been available at J. Pearson's General Merchandise for eight dollars.

FIFTEEN

I awoke at dawn for the twelfth time since retiring, famished and stiff. I hadn't eaten since noon yesterday, at a station stop where boiled beef and tinned peas made up the bill of fare, but I'd been too tired from the trip to venture out from the parsonage once I'd established residence. I was in possession of a new set of aches on top of those I'd acquired from the Overland. The bed needed slats and a mattress whose horse hair stuffing hadn't migrated to the outer edges. Someone — I learned later it was the fourteen-year-old son of one of the lay readers who had taken up the slack between pastors — had stocked the woodbox beside the stove; I built a fire, warmed a kettle I filled from the pump outside, and used it to freshen up and shave over an enamel dishpan that served as a basin, then finished dressing and went out to greet my first full day in Owen.

It greeted me back with a sixty-mile-an-hour gust, the first of many that had me chasing my old slouch hat across the Staked Plain all day long. You have to train a hat. I was sorry I'd left my regular one behind, even if the quality was too good for a penniless preacher. I wondered if a stampede string would look out of place on a pedestrian headpiece, but in the end I decided that the sight of a scarecrow leaning into the wind holding down the crown with one hand was humble enough to help the disguise.

I put my hunger to dual advantage and stepped into the Pan Handle, where the freight office clerk had told me I'd find Charlie Sweet helping out his sister while he recovered from his bullet wound. As I leaned the door shut against the gale from outside, the smell of hot grease scraped at my empty stomach. Six tables covered with oilcloth took up most of the space in the small room, leaving only a narrow crooked path for the server to pass carrying his steaming tray. Fortunately he was rail thin, and fresh-looking hollows in his cheeks suggested that the ordeal of recuperation had swindled him out of pounds he could ill spare. He walked with the stiff gait of a man with a bad back; that was where the bullet had entered, but from experience I gathered he was less concerned with pain than with preserving stitches. A pair of rugged boots stuck out beneath the hem of his long apron.

It was early, and only two tables were occupied. When he finished setting out plates of food on one, he turned my way with the empty tray under one arm. "Sit anyplace, Parson. You got your choice of sausage and eggs or eggs and sausage. Flapjacks if you like, but I wouldn't today: weevils in the batter."

"Sausage and eggs, then, please, and black coffee. Scrambled," I added. That was the easiest way to prepare eggs and Brother Bernard wasn't a man to create inconvenience.

He nodded curtly and pushed through a door that swung on a pivot into the sizzling chamber of the kitchen. I selected a table in a corner by a window to cut down on eavesdroppers. In less than five minutes, he returned bearing my order on the tray and a two-gallon coffeepot in the other hand. He put the plate in front of me, its contents still cooking furiously, and filled a thick stoneware mug with the densest, blackest brew I'd seen in more than a week. His face, which had lost much of what appeared to have been a lifelong burn, flushed deep copper in appreciation when I expressed pleasure at the sight.

"Mud's my department," he said. "Janey's Wild Bill with a skillet, but she never made coffee the same way twice in a row and always weak as a drownded kitten."

"I understand you're more accustomed to sitting on top of a stagecoach than waiting on tables."

"I am for a fact, and I'll be back up there soon. This ceiling's commencing to come down on me."

"Not too soon, I hope. I'm told a bullet wound is not a thing to rush healing."

He regarded me through eyesockets brambled with creases. Three inches of fair whiskers circled his lower face in the Mormon manner, but the tiny crucifix he wore at his throat supported the reports that he was a Roman Catholic. I'd begun to take note of such things. "You come educated. You the new fellow over at the Unitarian?"

"I got in yesterday. People have been most helpful in acquainting me with the community. I hope I didn't upset you with what I heard."

"There's no shame in getting shot. I intend to turn the shame on them that done it, soon as I'm in a position to. I reckon you'd say that's taking the Lord's own vengeance unto myself."

" 'Judge not lest ye be judged.' " I took a bite of sausage. It was spicier than I like it, but when I swallowed, the acids in my belly pounced on it like sitting prey. I wasn't looking at him. "Would you like to talk about it?"

"Well, Parson, I'm not just your denomination."

"You may think of me as a sympathetic stranger, and disregard the collar. I'm here to make friends, not poach on my neighbor's property."

He stroked the underside of the fringe on his chin. "You best tie in. That lard sets up like tar when it gets cold. I'll go see what's keeping them biscuits." He returned to the kitchen, stopping on the way to make sure the other diners were contented.

I ate my eggs, which were just right, and drenched my self-recrimination in the strong coffee. I'd come on just as strong and chased away my first best source of direct information on the Blue Bandannas, as I'd come to think of them.

Shortly after the door swung shut on him I heard raised voices, a man's and a woman's. They were hushed quickly and he came back out carrying three steaming bowls covered with checked cloths, one in his right hand, the other two lined up along his left arm from the crook of his elbow to the base of his palm. He set one on each of the other occupied tables, placed the third before me, drew out the chair facing me, and sat down.

"Janey's more of a chore to work for than Wells, Fargo," he said, taking a biscuit for himself, "but if blessed Mary had an oven, she couldn't bake better."

I took one and broke it apart. It was as light as a banknote and piping hot. I'd noticed there was no butter on any of the tables, but when I bit into it I realized why. It melted on my tongue. "The next time I encounter an atheist I'll send him here. He'll not question miracles again."

He winked, chewing. "We're powerful close to blaspheming here, Reverend. They're better than most, but they won't smuggle a sinner past Saint Peter."

"That was my hunger speaking, from its impiety. I missed supper." I had been ladling it out with a shovel; the mark was dangerous to fall short of, but just as bad to overshoot. I wiped my hands with my napkin and held one out, introducing myself. "Brother, not Reverend. I have no claim to any title not granted by the fraternity of man."

He took it in a palm ridged with calluses from the lines. "Circuit rider. Well, Father

198

Cress may not approve, but he's a thorny old bush. Charlie Sweet. Sweeney to friends and such."

"I hope to earn that honor. Are you much in pain since your ordeal?"

"It hurt worse coming out than it did going in. I'd be back in the traces by now if it wasn't for the risk I'd start bleeding again. Then it's three more weeks on my belly and Janey changing the dressing two times a day and calling me all kinds of a damn fool while she's about it. Pardon my language, Reverend — Brother. I ain't in gentle company so frequent." He crossed himself and popped the rest of his biscuit into his mouth.

"Have those men been captured?" I used mine to swab grease off my plate, putting concentration into it.

"They ain't, and it's thanks to the governor that's so. Now that the sheep trouble's let up, all he and the Rangers care about is what Pablo and Jose are up to down on the border. I say let 'em snatch a few head and stick up riders fool enough to carry more'n a cartwheel dollar that close to old Mexico. They'll just spend what they get in Texas, because there ain't a thing worth buying where they come from. Sow it around."

"One might say the same about the men

who waylaid you."

"No, sir, that's false. This bunch buries its money, or goes up to Denver or somesuch other place that needs it like a hen needs a pecker. Pardon my coarse language." He crossed himself again. "If I had a five-cent piece for every double eagle that showed up on a bar or a store counter anywhere in a hundred miles, I'd have a dime. I can abide a thief, though I'm pledged to lay down my hide to stop them in their taking ways and by God I will, but a miser's bad for business." He pardoned himself and made the sign a third time.

"What makes you think they're not still in Denver or someplace like that?"

"That fellow that told Randy to throw down the box had West Texas all through his speech. I heard that even laying on the ground with a slug in my back. You can't put that on, not when a West Texan's on the other end of it. You ever meet anyone from West Texas?"

"Not until I got here. I've led a sheltered life."

"Not the reason. You didn't on account of no West Texas boy ever leaves it for long. It gets in you like a tapeworm; you can't stay away even if you was wanted here for topping a nun." His theme had him so worked up he forgot to ask forgiveness from me or the pope. "He's here, count on it, and so's his crew. They rustled a thousand head of Herefords outside White Horse just last week."

Captain Jordan had said it was five hundred. Rumors seemed to grow faster in that arid soil than other places, but I wasn't supposed to know anything about the rustling so I didn't correct him. His was the first statement I'd heard that corroborated Judge Blackthorne's conviction that the gang operated close to home. "Did you tell the authorities the man was local?"

"I told everyone that bothered to listen, but it skidded off 'em like spit. Bad hats come from Missouri and Kansas and from down below the Rio Grande. Nobody wants to hear we're growing our own."

I doubted that was the reason. As far as I could tell he'd spoken of this to Texans exclusively, who might be expected to regard one of their own as less than sensitive to differences in dialect; but shotgun messengers crossed state and territorial lines and guarded passengers from all over the country. They might not be connoisseurs of geographical speech patterns, but they would know domestic from imported. "Why West? Don't all the natives of this state sound the same?"

"To you, maybe, but you're green. Much east of San Saba they could pass for Virginia, though not to a Virginian, like as not. I don't claim special powers, just good hearing."

"What about the driver; Randy, was that his name? Didn't he back you up?"

"Randy's from Connecticut originally. He thinks everyone talks funny once you get past New Haven."

"Does he live here in town?"

"His wife got spooked after the robbery and made him move to Louisiana and clerk in a freight office. You ask a lot of questions for a preaching man."

I could have played that two ways: emphasize my willingness to bring comfort to the stricken or fall back on Brother Bernard's past. I chose the one less holy. "I'm sorry to pry. This is the first time I've been more than five miles from where I was born. I'm overcome with the strangeness of it all. I never realized this country was so big."

He laughed then, and helped himself to another biscuit. I'd scored with his provincial pride. "Oh, well, Brother, if the panhandle's as big as you think it gets, wait till you take the train to El Paso. You can hide all of New England and most of Michigan between there and where we're sitting."

Other diners had begun to file in. The kitchen door opened and a woman nearly as thin as Sweet leaned in, wiping her hands on her apron. She stared at the back of his head until he turned her way, started, and rose. "Thanks for the palaver, Brother. It saved me scrubbing pots."

I stood and shook his hand again. "I can see you're both busy. I'd like to come by sometime and meet your sister."

"You wouldn't like it long. She lumps in Protestants with pagans and Chinamen."

I took out my wallet, but he stopped me with a palm. "Put it in the poor box on me," he said. "I'm not so certain as Janey. I like to back the other fellow's hand just in case."

I thanked him and left. I was in the right place, I was sure of that now. I just didn't know what for.

Sixteen

The First Unitarian Church of Owen was filled nearly to capacity that first Sunday, but having made few contacts during my brief time in town, I put it down less to personal impression than to plain curiosity. A medicine show or a company of dwarves would have filled the place as efficiently.

I'd committed a professional blunder early, when Mrs. McIlvaine hastened in at my first pull on the bell rope, flung down her broom, and seized the rope from my hands. No one had told me bell ringing was one of her duties, and from the alien serenity in her expression while she tugged away I concluded it was her favorite. She said not a word to me the rest of the day; which when you factored in how few she measured out all told made for a profound silence.

Almost all the pews were filled when Richard and Colleen Freemason arrived and walked all the way up the aisle without stopping to a space in front that had been conspicuously left vacant. He wore a black morning coat with piped lapels over a gray double-breasted waistcoat and gray trousers without a crease to indicate that it had ever spent time on a shelf with the ready-mades, she an unadorned velour dress with her hair gathered beneath a tricorne hat angled slightly with a small feather. The dress looked black until she crossed through a sunbeam slanting in through a window, when it proved to be a very dark maroon. Freemason shook the odd hand, scarcely slowing his pace. Standing at the pulpit, I took mental note of the hands he didn't shake because they weren't offered, and the faces that went with them; they were stony as a rule and turned straight ahead as he passed. In this way I managed to catalogue those acquaintances connected with or sympathetic to the cattle trade. Colleen kept her gaze forward. I remembered what the clerk in the Wells, Fargo office had said about her aloof reputation. That friendly fellow sat near the center of a pew halfway down, next to a woman close to his age whose expression was as grim as those of Freemason's enemies. I'd seen that same look on many female faces over the years when Colleen was present. The women were always respectable in appearance and nearly always less attractive.

When the couple was seated, Freemason with his banker's tile in his lap, I ventured a look from my notes and met Colleen's eyes, blue and cool and casually friendly, fully in keeping with the wife of a church director who wished the new pastor well on his first day. To this day she remains the best poker player I ever met, and I've played with Luke Short and Arnold Rothstein.

I broke contact to put my pages in order. I was as nervous as a cat. Everything Eldred Griffin had told me about when and where to pause, how often to look up, and where to look fled from memory. Speaking in an empty church to a stern taskmaster of a tutor had been unsettling; pretending wisdom of things spiritual before a packed house put bats in my stomach, and the certain knowledge that at least one of my listeners knew me for a fraud made my throat dry as Texas. I took too hearty a drink from the tumbler of water Mrs. McIlvaine had set out for me on the shelf beneath the lectern and had to fight back an explosive cough, which I covered by clearing my throat noisily into a fist. This was worse than facing a pistol in a hostile hand, because I knew what to do if mine misfired. There was nothing to duck behind that would spare me from scorn and only ignominious retreat through the side door for escape. I thought of Judge Blackthorne in his pew in the Presbyterian Church in Helena and wondered if he paused in his devotions to consider my situation and allow himself a smile with his cumbersome teeth.

I was wearing the fine shirt Esther Griffin had stitched for me with her husband's cutthroat collar, and had spent the previous evening brushing my coat and trousers and blacking my town shoes, which pinched and made me yearn for my good broken-in boots, but which at least distracted my attention from the terror of the moment. With unsteady fingers I opened my hymnal, as worn and grubby as any that had been placed in the racks, held it flat atop my notes, took a deep breath, and led the parishioners in a hymn. I've a strong voice and had been told I could sing without embarrassing myself unduly, but I was grateful for the baritones in the gallery that drowned out the wobble.

The hymn had a calming influence, as of course it was intended to; by the time the last stanza finished in the rafters I felt a little less like bolting. Someone coughed in the silence. I took that as my downstroke and began my sermon.

I'd moved the hymnal to the shelf beside the tumbler and brought up the Bible I'd carried from Montana Territory, opening it to the passage I'd marked with a strip I'd torn from the old newspaper lining the drawer in the parsonage. I wet my throat again — a small sip this time — and read:

" 'Now there was a day when the sons of God came to present themselves before the Lord, and Satan came also among them.

" 'And the Lord said unto Satan, Whence comest thou? Then Satan answered the Lord, and said, From going to and fro in the earth, and from walking up and down in it.

" 'And the Lord said unto Satan, Hast thou considered my servant Job, that there is none like him in the earth, a perfect and an upright man, one that feareth God, and escheweth evil?

" 'Then Satan answered the Lord, and said, Doth Job fear God for nought?

" 'Hast not thou made an hedge about him, and about his house, and about all that he hath on every side? Thou hast blessed the work of his hands, and his substance is increased in the land.

" 'But put forth thine hand now, and touch all that he hath, and he will curse thee to thy face.

" 'And the Lord said unto Satan, Behold, all that he hath is in thy power; only upon himself put not forth thine hand.' "

Hereupon I closed the book with as much reverberation as I could muster, wishing it were as substantial as the one in Griffin's study, which boomed like a rebel four-pounder when he slammed it shut. I was, however, aware of a sudden awakening in my audience; I'd been correct in guessing that the succession of lay readers who'd been putting them to sleep with rote had not deigned to depart from the text, and from the reaction I made bold to ponder whether the Reverend Rose had been in the practice of delivering sermons from his own hand. What I did wasn't heresy, not yet, but I felt an edge of uncertainty in the air, heavily tinged as it was with furniture oil and Sunday-suit mothballs, and uncertainty was something I knew a thing or two about.

"My friends," I said, "you know this story: In his desperation to turn Job against God and prove his point, Satan rustled his sheep and oxen, dropped a house on his seven sons and three daughters, and afflicted him with boils. Job was no more than mortal, complaining bitterly of his losses and his miseries, which he professed he had done nothing to bring upon him. But he maintained his faith in his Lord even when his wife counseled him to curse God and die, and so the Lord restored his chattel twofold, granted him seven new sons and three new daughters, and gave him twice his threescore and ten in years as a reward for his unshakeable faith while Satan crept away beaten, with his forked tail tucked between his legs."

To illustrate this image, which does not appear in the Book of Job, I walked two fingers across the top of the pulpit, staggering a little. Amusement rippled through the crowd. I let it die down, then continued.

"Some would say that God was flattering Himself when He declared that justice had been rendered unto His servant, that seven new sons and seven new daughters did not replace the lives of the first seven sons and three daughters, and that doubling the span of Job's days denied him reunion with those he had lost at the end of his threescore and ten. They're right, of course."

That drew a gasp and a murmur, but I was concentrating on Colleen, who met my gaze with polite interest, nothing more. It was as if we hadn't discussed the subject only the day before yesterday.

I said, "One sheep looks pretty much like another, and an ox is just a steer broken to harness. Even Charles Goodnight would be hard pressed to distinguish between two longhorns standing side by side." More chuckles. Goodnight had brought prosperity to the region when he established his ranch near Palo Duro Canyon, and was a popular subject locally. "Children are another matter. Nothing but the resurrection of Job's original sons and daughters would serve as adequate compensation for his sufferings.

"God knew this. He wept for Job's great loss, and rendered unto him the only justice available; for there can be but one mortal resurrection in the Holy Book, and that must be performed by His son."

I rearranged my pages, pretending to read them. I'd committed the text solidly to memory. I looked up and smiled. "Owen has been kind to this pilgrim, cleansing him and giving him bread and protecting his small heap of belongings, refusing to accept anything in return. Nowhere have I seen greater evidence of faith in God. I'm told that before I came, this country had been afflicted with range wars and highwaymen, stricken by murderers and forsaken by those who were pledged to keep it from evil. Yet you welcomed a stranger not with suspicion or malice, but with love. And so Satan has lost again, and must go to and fro in the earth in search of some other victim to prove his false theory; for the Book of Owen is a work still in progress."

There was no applause, naturally, but when I called for another hymn, the house responded with energy, basses booming, sopranos trilling, and the inevitable tone-deaf howls enthusiastic. It wasn't exactly the equivalent of a standing ovation, but I had the impression I'd passed my first test. I added points by bringing the services to a close after reading the community announcements I'd been given and reciting the forty-first psalm.

I took my place beside the door to the street as the parishioners filed out, shaking hands with the men and bowing to the women. My notices were mostly positive, although one red-faced fellow who'd slept through most of the morning, stirring just long enough to hear me refer to myself as a pilgrim, expressed the opinion that I should have withheld Plymouth Rock until Thanksgiving. An old woman in rusty weeds told me she wished her husband had lived to hear me speak, and spent five minutes cataloguing his trials while others grew impatient and left the line behind her.

Richard Freemason took my hand in his

iron grip; either he was accustomed to dealing with politicians or Captain Jordan had been mistaken when he'd called him a gentleman rancher. Poking letters into pigeonholes is poor exercise for the hands.

"I felt I'd made a good choice in you when we met," he said. "It's a pleasure to have that feeling confirmed."

"Thank you, sir. I had misgivings about the references to sheep and cattle."

"Those wars are finished, and subtlety is lost on Texas. You should publish."

"I wouldn't presume."

"Nonsense. I have some acquaintances in publishing, who may have some contacts with the ecclesiastical press. I'll give you a recommendation."

I thanked him, and found his wife's gloved hand in mine. "Wherever did you find your inspiration?" Her smile carried no trace of mockery.

"I found it in a charming new acquaintance, Mrs. Freemason," I said. If she wanted to broach the subject in the presence of her husband, I wouldn't back away. "I came with a bundle of sermons, but none was appropriate to our discussion. I promised you a sermon in return for your gracious hospitality, you may remember."

Freemason said, "The story of Job is one

of Colleen's bugbears. I'd no idea you two had dissected theology at the house."

"Brother Bernard is very approachable, dear. I won't say he's converted me to the God of the Old Testament, but he makes an excellent case for the defense. One might think he knew his way around the halls of justice." She'd made a bargain not to expose me. Nothing had been said about torture.

I put a smile on my face I hoped was modest. "My father was a deacon. One of his happiest entertainments was to engage me in religious discourse from the time I was old enough to read scripture."

"My father was a butcher in Manchester," Freemason said. "I can't recall a single intelligent conversation I ever had with him. Tell me, Brother, with which church was your father affiliated?"

I'd made a mistake in volunteering a detail from Sebastian's manufactured past. Now I hesitated to provide specific information that could be exploded by a simple inquiry.

Colleen, of all people, came to my rescue. She placed a hand on his arm. "Dear, we mustn't monopolize the brother. Others are waiting to speak with him."

"Of course. Mrs. Freemason and I would be honored to have you in for dinner. Will you be free this afternoon?"

"I'm honored to accept." There was nothing for it but to open myself to further inquisition. Inventing an excuse wasn't an option. I've always found it difficult to tell a white lie while I was living a direct falsehood.

"Splendid! Two o'clock."

Colleen's smile was angelic. That was when she was at her most diabolical. She gave me a nod and left on her husband's arm.

By the time the church doors closed I had three more invitations to dine that week. Returning to the parsonage, I locked the door, opened my valise, took out the bottle of Old Forester I'd brought from Helena, and helped myself to a secular swig.

Seventeen

"My mother was American," Richard Freemason said. "Still is, I suspect, although we haven't spoken in ten years. She's never forgiven me for deserting her for the frontier, but since she always cashes the bank draughts I send her in Boston, she hasn't wasted away from a broken heart. I'm a man, and therefore unworthy of her trust. I have my father to thank for that. He proposed to her in London while she was taking the Grand Tour with her parents, representing himself as the owner of a chain of meatpacking plants that exported abroad, but after a wedding trip to Brighton she learned he had only the one shop and his most distant customer lived six squares away. She divorced him when I was five and brought me with her back to the States. Evidently, having made one disastrous decision on the spur of the moment, she was determined to take her time arriving at the second."

"And was that disastrous as well?" I sat back to give Fielo, the venerable Mexican manservant, room to ladle chowder into my shallow china bowl. Ocean fish was an almost nonexistent delicacy in West Texas.

"Eventually, but I had a hand in how it turned out. My grandparents furnished her with an annuity to help rear me until age eighteen. I leapt the fence at fifteen, and when they found out they cut her off without a penny. She made me aware of that fact in her response to a letter I sent months later, bringing her up to date on my experiences since quitting the maternal nest. That was our last exchange. She's never sent me so much as an acknowledgment for the money I send regularly — have done, since I got my first job stocking shelves in a dry goods in St. Louis. Her bank takes care of that by providing the canceled draughts with her signature on the back."

"Still," I said, "you have kept the Fifth Commandment. That speaks well of you."

"It speaks better of Colleen, who insisted I continue after I expressed the opinion that I had paid the old lady sufficient rent for the time I spent in her womb."

Colleen shook her head when the old man arrived at her place with his tureen. He

217

served Freemason and returned to the kitchen. "As with bold entrepreneurs the world over," she said, "odious rumors follow Richard everywhere he goes. The monthly emolument is a small price to pay to avoid accusations of abandoning his own mother."

That was vanity and a sin, but I forebore to point it out. Griffin had drilled into me the importance of not preaching to one's hosts. Furthermore it was a lie. Colleen had climbed to a precarious level where her past balanced delicately against her current claim to respectability. Whispers that she'd bewitched her husband into maintaining her in luxury while his mother starved would make her an expensive liability if he intended to increase his grip on the panhandle (if that was his aim; I hadn't gotten his measure yet). To an extent, her true motives exonerated her. The Bible says nothing against taking action in one's own defense.

The dining room was small by the standards of that type of house, but seemed spacious by way of its lack of fussy detail. It contained none of the porcelain bric-a-brac and lace and velvet drapery that turned large Eastern salons into crowded airless warehouses where you had to plan your entrances and exits beforehand to avoid knocking over some favorite piece of gim-crack. The rectory table was less than ten feet long and stood on four handsomely turned legs atop a rug of Old World manu-facture with both halves of the globe em-broidered in its center, with five of the full set of shieldback chairs placed against the walls and a massive sideboard carved from fruitwood where additional courses could be placed to keep the serving apparatus operating smoothly during larger affairs than ours. Good landscapes hung in gilt frames and a crystal chandelier built on the modest scale of the room were the only ornaments in sight. I sensed the hand of the lady of the house in the decoration. She would march resolutely in the opposite direction of the gold-etched mirrors, glisten-ing mahogany, and dripping bronze barbar-ity of the saloons where she'd made her liv-ing before she found an easier way.

The food was excellent, and in keeping with the room's quiet taste. After the chow-der we ate roasted breast of duckling in a light cream sauce, asparagus in butter, sweet potatoes, warm moist bread (in my experi-ence second only to Jane Sweet's biscuits at the Pan Handle restaurant), and finished with mincemeat pie and coffee poured from an oriental silver decanter. The cook, Freemason said, had come from Belgium to open a tearoom with her husband in New York City, only to lose him to fever during the voyage. The sheepman had discovered her slinging delicately seasoned stew in a bunkhouse full of ranch hands who wouldn't know fennel from feather grass and appropriated her to serve as his personal chef. The coffee was as good as Charlie Sweet's, refined probably with eggshells without recourse to the mythical properties so many amateur brewers assign to chicory.

I was relaxed, but on my guard. That medicinal jolt of whiskey had flattened my nerves and I had a story ready in case Freemason pressed the point of my fictional father's church: The fires that had plagued Denver until an ordinance was passed requiring all new construction to be made of brick had claimed any number of such institutions, an excuse I hoped would retard the process of confirmation long enough for me to finish my work in Owen. He didn't ask, however. He seemed more concerned with how much part the First Unitarian church might play in the progress of civilization in the region. Primarily he sought assurance that the railroad would come to town instead of bypassing it for White Horse or some other point, leaving Owen to dry up and blow away before the incessant wind from Arizona.

"Please don't be offended when I tell you there was resistance to appointing an evangelist to the pastorship," he said, stirring sugar into his cup. "Some members of the board of directors opposed the, er, rootlessness of your particular denomination. I reminded them that solid Unitarianism had done nothing to slow the erosion every time the Reverend Rose served up one of his tasteless homilies from Numbers. Surely there is no other book that so thoroughly replicates the effect of reading a shopkeeper's inventory."

I smiled. "Fifty and three thousand and four hundred of the children of Naphtali, six hundred thousand and three thousand and five hundred and fifty of the children of Israel, threescore and two thousand and seven hundred of the children of Dan. I confess that I could never satisfy myself as to the correct total of my mother's household accounts until I arrived at the same sum three times. I must own that my reason for trying to put life in my sermons is not entirely selflessness. It's important for a minister to set a good example by staying awake at the pulpit."

"And so you did. And so did the congregation, mostly." He'd been seated in front of the red-faced parishioner who'd snored his way through most of the service from the first hymn to the last "Amen." "I daresay you bought me some credibility with the rest of the board this morning. The true test will come next Sunday, when we learn the amount of attrition now that native curiosity is satisfied."

"You may concern yourself with other things, Richard. Brother Bernard is no flash in the pan."

I looked at the lady of the house, sipping her coffee black from a cup so thin I could see the contrast between the contents and its surface. I wasn't looking for any sign of dissembling, because I knew they wouldn't show. After the journey through the bleak landscape of the Cimmaron Strip and what lay south of it, I owed myself the pleasure of the sight. It was no wonder Freemason had disregarded the disadvantages of her life story in order to place her at the head of his table.

Not precisely the head; the couple observed the egalitarian practice of sitting not at opposite ends of the refectory piece, but side by side in the middle, facing their guest. Butcher's son that he was (and whatever else he may have been, robber baron or murderer or festering thorn in Judge Blackthorne's thick hide), he had a gift for politics. That was as important a trait in a ranching pioneer as rough justice and vision.

"Other concerns indeed," said he, and when I turned my attention back to him there was no indication on his face that the conversation had been light until then. "The sheep wars are finished, barring the odd inevitable flare-up, but these bandits must be addressed. Railroad builders think nothing of blasting their way through miles of granite, but a series of disconnected raids can force them to change their course by a hundred miles. I know you've heard about our late troubles in that area. You had breakfast yesterday with Charlie Sweet."

I was careful there. The palmists may have been right: Give a man or a thing a moment's thought in some company and it's the same as saying the name aloud. "I didn't see you there."

"I wasn't; Madame Lemonnier's ducklings and pastries have spoiled me for the beans and bacon in the Pan Handle. It's a small town still, and that collar stands out. By now, half the population's convinced you've converted Sweeney from Roman idolatry, if not his formidable sister."

It was as much a question as a statement, and I took my time chewing and swallowing a mouthful of pie before I answered. "I'd heard about the stagecoach robbery when I stopped in Wichita Falls. The clerk in the freight office here gave me more details. When I found out Mr. Sweet was the man serving me breakfast, I inquired about his health. I've learned that talking about such things brings comfort."

"Taking action against them brings surcease. Sometimes I think the raids are not disconnected after all, and that these brigands have set themselves to drive me to ruin."

"You're being melodramatic," Colleen said. "You suffered direct losses in three of the raids, but not all. Considering the amount of business you do, and how dependent it is upon the railroads, you make a broad target."

"In a way I'm connected to them all. When they hit their first train they made off with my payroll. The second was carrying securities I'd borrowed from my bank in Chicago to repair the loss. The cattle they rustled at White Horse were purchased from Goodnight to trade in Colorado for breeding stock to improve my wool yield. I've suffered more than anyone from these raids, and if the railroad bypasses Owen because of them, I'll be a pauper. I confess, Brother, to envying Job at one point during your sermon. My faith is not so stalwart."

I resisted reminding him that Sweet and the cowhand slain at White Horse may have suffered as much. "If Job's convictions were less rare, I'd have no work."

Colleen said, "You might chide him for the sin of pride. Not every misfortune takes place with him in mind."

"I wouldn't presume, in his own house. I trust pains were taken to keep secret the details of how the valuables were being transported."

Freemason's bulbous forehead gathered in bunches. "They were known to no one but my representatives, myself, and the people I do business with. Are you suggesting a Judas?"

"I'm unqualified to suggest it. I'm unschooled in the ways of the world, and too curious for comfort. Please accept my apologies."

He lifted his cup to his lips. "Sometimes innocent eyes see clearest. Lord knows my garden is crawling with serpents."

Colleen said, "Perhaps the Brother suspects Eve."

I made so bold as to intercept her gaze,

but it lingered less than an instant before turning to her husband, who made a dry sound in his throat and patted her hand. "My dear, I'd sooner suspect the Brother of an indiscretion." He returned to his reflections. "If I find this serpent and sever its head, another will take its place. I've beseeched the governor to send us a company of Rangers, but it appears I exhausted all my goodwill in Austin when he agreed to support the fence-cutting law." He set down his cup for refilling by Fielo, who'd appeared behind his left shoulder. "I admit I hadn't considered the possibility of a breech in my wall. That suggests a single enemy. I wonder which one."

Colleen said, "Find the breech and trace it to its source."

"But where to start?"

"Coffee, Señor?" The old Mexican hovered over me with the decanter.

■ ■ ■ ■ ■

III
THE BOOK OF JUDAS

■ ■ ■ ■ ■

EIGHTEEN

Colleen reminded Freemason he had work waiting and insisted on seeing me to the door. He shook my hand and withdrew to his study as she looped her arm inside mine. It felt pleasant, even if the last time she'd done that was just before someone had tried yet again to kill me.

"You came all this way to break up a gang of common bandits?" She spoke low. People who keep servants do as a rule.

"I didn't say that."

"You didn't have to. Richard is the second person in town you've spoken to about the robberies. You have no outside interests, Page. You're quite dull when you come down to it."

"We can't all be as inspirational as Brother Bernard."

"I'm not your spy. I've more to gain by being loyal to my husband than by robbing him."

"You said yourself he's gone bust."

"I've seen busted from both sides. His kind has a different definition. When he hasn't ten cents for a shave he can raise a million dollars on his reputation. There ought to be another word for that kind of busted."

"There is. It's called running a bluff. All the more reason to hit him for the hard cold cash he gets up that way."

"I'm not like that anymore."

I laughed. "I don't believe it. No one ever accused you of being dull."

"I'm serious. You get awfully tired dealing from the bottom of the deck. You start to wonder if the suckers are right and the game's more fun if you play it according to Hoyle."

"You wouldn't know Hoyle if he bet his watch and chain against the pot."

We'd reached the door. She looked up at me. Her eyes were as clear as flakes of sky. How they stayed that way when they were attached to Colleen Bower's brain stumped me worse than the Infinite. "I'd suspect you of personal motives if I thought you ever had human qualities," she said. "Did I break your heart?"

"You as much as said I don't have one."

"Someone broke mine long before we

met, and you know something? You can still feel the pain in a leg after it's been cut off and buried."

"What about the house boy? He's old enough to start thinking about a pension."

"Fielo belongs to an old aristocratic family wiped out by Juaristas in the revolution. He fought for his country in the Mexican War, only to lose everything, including a son, after Maximilian fell twenty years later. He came here with nothing but the rags on his back and a ferocious hatred for all *bandidos*. He wouldn't lift a finger to help out the Yankee variety. Anyway, he's frail, his duties aren't physically demanding, and Richard pays him nearly as much as his top hand on the ranch. I asked him to. I doubt the old fellow would take the risk."

"I'd like to visit the ranch. Can you arrange it?"

"So it's the gang you're after."

"Yes. Are you happy now that you got me to say it?"

"The word is relieved. I wanted to make sure you weren't acting as Blackthorne's avenging angel."

"What happened between Freemason and the Judge?"

"Ask the Judge." She opened the door and held it.

"What about the ranch?"

"Shall I say you're eager to bring the godless hands into the fold?"

"Tell him Brother Bernard wishes to know more of the world."

"And if he responds that he wishes to know more of Brother Bernard?"

"He won't. I accepted this invitation to give his people time to search the parsonage. I hid my traveling bottle in the outhouse and left a letter from Bernard's sweet dead mother where they wouldn't have to look too hard to find it."

Her face drew taut over its very good bones. "Only a deeply corrupt man would suspect such corruption of a man he'd met only twice."

"Avenging angels don't get haloes. The man who taught me my gospel made that clear."

He hadn't trusted the job to someone clumsy from the bunkhouse. If I hadn't purposely left the drawer in the nightstand slightly ajar and done some other things to provide tells that someone had been through the place, I'd have thought no one had entered it from the time I left until the time I returned. Mrs. McIlvaine had Sunday afternoon off, to do whatever it was she did when she stood her broom in its shallow closet in the church, so I was fairly certain she hadn't been in to clean. The counterfeit letter containing Sebastian's brief biography was where I'd placed it, folded under the brass lamp on the nightstand with his mother's tintype leaning against its base, but the lamp was turned slightly. That pointed to a literate intruder who'd taken down the information to report to his employer.

It being Sunday, I was sure a communication would be going out to Denver by tomorrow's Overland, seeking to confirm the letter's sparse details. Blackthorne never confided the nature of his intelligence organization to subordinates; I had to assume that whoever had handled Sebastian's telegraph exchange with Freemason was in charge of such follow-ups, but I didn't trust him, or for that matter anyone else who held my fate in his hands. I had only the hope that the vague wording of the letter on the nightstand would slow down the inevitable long enough for me to get what I needed and make away. Since that involved pumping the Judge for the details of his past relationship with Freemason, I propped myself up in the iron bed with a writing

block on my knees and drafted the following message:

Dear Mr. Smith,

I've been in Owen days only and everyone I've met has gone to great lengths to
make me feel important. Although I confess to homesickness, it is, I'm convinced,
God's will that I am in a place where I
know my work is useful and wanted.
Already I flatter myself that I have brought
comfort to the afflicted. Mr. Freemason's
confidence in my humble gifts is re-
assuring and gives me strength to believe
that nothing I did in the past is a tenth part
of the good that my service to the Lord will
accomplish here. All that came before is
prelude to the hard work and sleepless
nights put to the purpose of bringing light
to Texas.

Please accept my sincere thanks for
your kindness to a stranger.

Yours in faith,
Bernard Sebastian

I smudged up several sheets, counting
words, striking some out, and adding others, before I had a draft I could transcribe
in proper penmanship and put aside to mail
by way of the Overland to Mr. J. Smith in

care of General Delivery in Wichita Falls. Captain Jordan, who'd assured me there were upwards of two dozen "J. Smiths" in town and among the ranches and settlements within plausible riding distance, had a standing agreement with the postmaster to hold all missives thus addressed for his scrutiny. Together we'd worked out a code that would enable me to write what appeared to be a harmless communication to some random brief friendly acquaintance while putting the Texas Rangers to service to the federal court. It was a simple enough cypher, but with sufficient room provided for to drench it in homely verbiage: After the greeting, every twentieth word conveyed the actual message. If it was urgent and assistance was required immediately and in force, I would begin with "My dear Mr. Smith"; otherwise, I was asking Jordan to forward the actual text by Western Union to Blackthorne. I had written:

important know Freemason's past before Texas

After placing the letter in the nightstand drawer where I didn't care who found it if I happened to become separated from it, I got up and fed the scribbled sheets to the fire in the laundry stove. I'd taken all the precautions I could, without feeling one bit more secure than I had before I'd written it. I don't place much trust in encryptions, on the theory that what one or two men could create, one or two others could dismantle. Carrier pigeons had at least the advantage of passing through no human hands between dispatch and delivery, but the thought that my life depended on a creature that spent most of its time from one mission to the next picking lice from its feathers was worse than knowing that the number of people who were in on my masquerade would fill out the regimental band at Fort Custer, with the last person I'd trust with either my wallet or my hide sharing a bed and who knew how many secrets with the man whose measure I was trying to take.

It was enough to drive a God-fearing man to drink. I was weighing the relative risk of retrieving the whiskey bottle from the outhouse when someone knocked on the door of the parsonage. I reached for my collar, then decided to leave it off and went through the sitting room with my sleeves rolled up and a towel from the dishpan–wash basin over my arm, the Deane-Adams concealed inside its folds.

At first glance I thought the man on my front step was Freemason, but then I saw the frock coat was too large for the visitor's slight frame and the silk hat rested too low on his forehead, bending down his ears, and knew him for Fielo, the aged house boy, wearing his master's castoff. He removed the hat, cradling it with a forearm, and held out an envelope with the Masonic compass-and-square embossed on the flap.

I laid the towel with the revolver rolled inside it on the rocking chair and took the envelope. The note was an invitation from Richard Freemason to accompany him to his ranch Tuesday at dawn. I asked the old man to take my acceptance to him with thanks. He bowed, turned, replaced the hat, and applied himself to the long walk back down the street and the steep climb up the limestone steps to the castle on the hill. He wasn't as frail as Colleen made out.

NINETEEN

Unexpectedly, I found my suspicions confirmed — or at least supported — the next
morning, when the door to the freight office
opened away from my hand and I was face
to face once again with Fielo, who hesitated,
raised and lowered his hand-me-down silk
hat, and stepped past me onto the boardwalk. There were any number of reasons
why the manservant of a busy ranch owner
would have business with a stagecoach line,
but I was satisfied that he'd just posted a
letter to Denver on Freemason's behalf to
test Brother Bernard's story.

It was Monday and a coach stood ready
before the door. That meant a waiting line
inside and I joined it. Luther Cherry, looking every bit the scarecrow I'd met during
the trip from Wichita Falls, in a morning
coat plastered with lint and stray hairs,
stood at the head of the line, arguing with
the friendly clerk behind the counter.

"Four-fifty just to carry a letter to St. Louis? I might as well pay a little more and deliver it in person."

"I'm sorry, sir; that's the special delivery rate. Undoubtedly it will come down after they string a telegraph line from Wichita Falls. It always does — competition, you understand. But that won't happen until after the railroad comes through."

"Until which time, Wells, Fargo will behave as arrogantly as any of the Eastern trusts. My God, I could buy a decent suit of clothes and pocket fifty cents!"

Clearly this invited a suggestion, but being affable by nature the clerk made another. "Regular delivery is two dollars, if you don't mind it taking an extra day or so."

"That won't do." Muttering to himself, the lawyer produced four banknotes from a lank wallet and laid them on the counter, then snapped open a Scotchman's coin purse and placed a twenty-five-cent piece, two dimes, and a nickel on top of them. The man behind the counter transferred them to a cash box, stamped a postmark on a long envelope in front of him, and poked it into a pigeonhole at his elbow.

On his way to the door, Cherry, grumbling still, nearly passed me without looking up.

"Life in the wilderness is not as reasonably priced as it was centuries ago, Mr. Cherry," I said.

"Indeed it is not, friend." He recognized me then and halted. "Good morning, Brother. I worked late Saturday night and overslept the next day, missing your sermon. I heard it brought down the house."

"Hardly that, but the reception was most kind."

"I'm sorry you overheard that altercation. I miss my wife, but if I continue to communicate with her at these rates I won't be able to afford her fare." He glanced down at the envelope in my hand. "I hope your people are patient. The Overland is no place for a man sworn to poverty."

"Fortunately, I made a new friend in Wichita Falls. The collection plate won't suffer mortally."

He was only half listening, preoccupied with the hands of his nicked watch. Presently he apologized for the demands of his workload, said good-bye, and took his leave.

When my turn came I handed the clerk my letter to Mr. J. Smith and paid its freight from the loose change in my pocket. He bent my ear over the excellence of the Sunday services until the people behind me began to clear their throats and shuffle their feet. A man tipped his hat and a woman dipped her chin as I walked past. I touched my brim to both. I understood then, a little, about the seductive nature of the Call. Edwin Booth was no more celebrated a figure on the streets of Chicago and San Francisco than a minister in a desert settlement.

Dawn comes early in flat country. I'd just entered the church Tuesday, carrying my second cup of cowboy coffee (paint stirrer required) when the creak of a harness drew me to the door. A Brewster-green Stanhope stood on red wheels beside the boardwalk, hitched to a round-bottomed sorrel with the shoulders of a Percheron; and good job, because it was pulling two passengers already.

Freemason, in a duster and flat-brimmed Stetson, sat holding the lines behind Luther Cherry. Today the sad-faced lawyer wore a straw hat and sturdy tweeds, out at the elbows but a happier union than his town coat. He clutched a battered leather briefcase on his lap and held down his flapping hat with his other hand against a mild forty-mile-an-hour wind. As I climbed aboard, he pressed in close to the driver to make room on a seat properly built for two.

"Another good morning to you, Brother,"

he said. "I apologize for the close quarters. I had a question about the boundaries, and Mr. Freemason was gracious enough to invite me to the ranch to see them for myself. No doubt you're growing tired of me by now."

He was a drab companion, and I've never warmed to skinflints, but I protested the opposite. Surreptiously I wedged my arm between us to keep him from pressing against the revolver in its scabbard. I didn't want to take the chance of Mrs. McIlvaine finding it in the parsonage, and in any case I wasn't about to venture into open country unarmed.

Freemason measured out a smile of contrition. "I yielded to an impulse. The cabriolet is at the ranch, and all the two-seaters are out on hire from the livery. I had this rig built to my order, so it's sound, and Bess is accustomed to hauling furniture in tandem, but by the time we cross the river I fear we'll be on rather more intimate terms with one another than we bargained for."

I said, "I don't mind. Mr. Cherry's presence shortened my journey here."

"A fine piece of fortune," said the sheepman. "I engaged both of you sight unseen, on the strength of my judge of character. Cherry clerked in the St. Louis firm that handled most of my transactions. When he passed the bar with applied study in real property, I retained him immediately. The man's knowledge is worth ten miles of fence."

The lawyer laughed. "If I may speak for Brother Bernard as well as for myself, it's handy there's just the one seat. You might otherwise have been tempted to bring along our friend the wire drummer, and expose us all to an exhaustive lecture on the relative merits of Glidden versus Reynolds, and whether Sunderland's Kink is as effective a deterrent as the Brink Twist."

"I've had my life's portion of those fellows." Our host released the brake and gave the lines a flip; Bess rolled her haunches and we were in motion. "They make no distinction between the walrus hide of a bull and the tender membrane of a ewe. Great patches of scar tissue are as devastating to the harvest of wool as blight to corn. Barbs are designed to contain cattle, dumb brutes that wander away from sure feed to graze on dead thistle in the desert. A week-old lamb knows better than that. No doubt Bo Peep abused her flock." No hint of a smile cracked his countenance.

I changed hands on my hat and shouted across the wind. "If you don't mind my asking, why, then, did you lobby so hard to strengthen the fence-cutting law?"

"Not to keep sheep in, you can be sure of that. I fought for it in order to keep the damn cattlemen out."

At length we crossed Wild Horse Creek at a point where deep ruts left by other vehicles marked the ford. The waters had just begun to recede from the spring runoff, and lapped at our hubs. When we rolled up the bank on the other side, the big mare shrugged, sprinkling us all. "A second baptism," offered Cherry.

For a mile or so we rode alongside four strands of wire strung between crazy crooked scrubwood posts that any rancher in good timberland would have scorned in favor of straight pine or cedar, while the tough short stubble of buffalo grass gradually gave ground to a lush expanse of bluestem nearly three feet high, ideal for grazing. Freemason had chosen his location well. The relentless wind combed the tops in hypnotic waves, like the pattern on the surface of an inland ocean. I directed my gaze away from it toward the level horizon to keep from becoming drunk on the sight. The grasses of the High Plains are proof that you can get seasick on dry land.

I spotted the horse and man in the road

first, just ahead of the rancher, who stiffened at the sight. The man was out of the saddle and kneeling near the fence in the attitude of cutting the wire. Freemason leaned forward and drew a brass-receiver Winchester from the footboards at the base of the seat onto his lap. This alerted Cherry.

"What a place to come bang up," he said. "It's lucky for him we happened along."

Trust a lawyer to size up a situation at one glance. I could see then that the man was too far from the fence to threaten it. At first I thought his horse had thrown a shoe, but as we drew near I saw that the man down on one knee with his back turned toward us was scraping at its right forefoot with a knife, paring the hoof or prying at a stone or some other object that had gotten wedged inside the iron. Our host relaxed, loosening his grip on the pistol stock of the repeater.

"Need help, friend?" he called out.

The man spun on his knee without rising, cocking and leveling a long-barreled Colt at Freemason across the crook of his right arm. He wore a gray hat, range flannels, and a blue bandanna that covered the lower half of his face.

My reflexes were a split second faster than the rancher's; my hand made an entirely involuntary move toward the revolver under my coat, but I stopped it through sheer force of will before it had covered a half inch. The masked man was concentrating on Freemason, who snatched at the carbine across his lap. The Colt flamed and something struck a post holding up the Stanhope's canvas roof. Freemason abandoned the Winchester to seize the lines and calm Bess.

The report seemed to serve double duty as a signal. From the fence and road, the grass-covered ground sloped gently toward the river, forming a shaggy apron some thirty feet wide between hardpack and water. In one smooth motion, a handful of horses scrambled to their feet, seeming to rise from the earth itself as if on hinges and levitating riders into their saddles.

I was more impressed than frightened. It takes more than just good horsemanship to keep eight hundred pounds of nervous animal down on its side without snorting or tossing a head or a tail; two hands are hardly enough to keep it calm and its nostrils covered and man and horse hidden in grass not much more than knee high, and simple athletic ability alone won't let him rise with it, slipping one foot into the stirrup and swinging the other leg over its back in the

same movement, man and beast uniting as
one. It was like something out of Revelation:

The first beast was like a lion, and the
second beast like a calf, and the third
beast had a face as a man, and the fourth
beast was like a flying eagle.
  And the four beasts had each of them
six wings about him; and they were full
of eyes within . . .

Only there were five beasts, clad in pale
dusters, gray hats, and blue bandannas, and
when the man in the road swung aboard his
horse, the muzzle of his revolver remaining
on point like the needle of a compass, we
faced six armed men, the others kneeing
their mounts forward until they formed a
half circle about us with weapons in hand.
  A sharp double-clack rang out across the
wind, and I turned my head as a seventh
rider cantered our way from Freemason's
property on the other side of the fence with
a fresh round levered into a Spencer rifle.
He wore the uniform of the pack, a strip of
tanned and weathered face showing between
the top of his bandanna and the brim of his
hat.
  "What does the Good Book say about

seven angels?" Cherry asked me in a low voice.

"These aren't angels."

Ten yards from the fence, the newcomer shouted and smacked his reins across his horse's withers, breaking it into gallop. It closed the distance in seconds and left the earth with no more apparent effort than a balloon rising, clearing the top strand of wire with inches to spare and braking to a halt short of the road, forelegs stiff and its rider leaning back on the reins, the repeater cradled along his right forearm.

Cherry did a foolish thing. Startled by the feat of athletic horsemanship and the thud of the landing, he shifted on the seat and his briefcase slid from his lap. He lunged to catch it. The Spencer bellowed and there was one less lawyer in Texas.

TWENTY

Something hot and wet splashed the back of my left hand; it was Luther Cherry's blood as he arched his back upon impact, then sagged against me with all his weight. He was breathing, but the nasty sucking sound meant a shot lung and a short life.

For me, there was no harnessing my instincts. Bess tried to rear between the traces, occupying both of Freemason's hands and all of his concentration. The Deane-Adams was in my right hand pointed at the man with the Spencer before I could give any thought to the action.

Six hammers and the lever of the repeater crackled across the wind. Facing seven muzzles, I let the revolver fall to the floorboards and raised my palms to my shoulders.

I was conscious of Freemason's eyes on me, leveled across Cherry's bent frame.

For five minutes — it was more likely

seconds — only the wind stirred. Then the man with the Spencer jerked his head at the rider nearest me, who nudged his mount alongside the buggy, leaned over to slide the Winchester off Freemason's lap, and tossed it to another rider nearby, who caught it one-handed. He scooped up the Deane-Adams and examined it, then flipped it toward the man with the Spencer. The Helena baseball team could have used that bunch in the infield.

"Check out the satchel."

The lawyer's briefcase was opened and its contents dumped out. Papers fluttered in every direction like bats flushed from a cave. The rider shook his head and dropped it in the road.

"Nice iron for a plug-hat preacher." The man with the Spencer raised my weapon and sighted down the barrel at a point between my eyes. His voice carried above the wind with the ease of someone accustomed to raising it, with a West Texas accent as flat as the panhandle. I was convinced he was the man Charlie Sweet had heard giving the orders during the Overland robbery. "Too good anyway for potting snakes and such."

"He's right handy with it, too." The man who'd picked it up had marbles in his

250

mouth, or more practically a cud in his cheek.

I said nothing. I could feel the muzzle on me as if it were pressing against the bridge of my nose.

At length the Spencer man lowered it, shook the shells out of the cylinder, and flipped the revolver back my way. That was a surprise, but I kept my hands where they were while it dropped at my feet with a clunk; it might have been a trick to make me grab for it and claim self-defense, with Freemason to furnish eyewitness testimony. Frontier courts didn't always mess with complications like an unloaded firearm.

"What do you want?" asked the rancher, speaking up for the first time. "I don't have much cash on me, and you can't break up my watch seven ways."

"We don't want your money, sheepman. We thought you was a payroll wagon."

"You know me?"

"I can smell you." He nodded to the man who'd disarmed us, who jacked all the shells out of the Winchester and slid it across the buggy's floorboards.

"Why so generous?" Freemason asked.

"Can't use the weight. Comes a choice betwixt gold and iron, I choose gold." He socked the Spencer into a scabbard slung from his saddle horn and gathered his reins. "You best get help for your friend, for what good it does. He was green or he'd know better than to jump like a jackrabbit when there's guns about."

He backed his horse off the road, then wheeled, followed closely by the others, in the direction we'd been headed. They bent low, raking their spurs for speed, billows of dust erupting from their horses' heels. We could see them a long time before they turned south away from the road and shrank from sight. Then a moan from Cherry brought us back to more urgent matter.

"He'll never make it to town," Freemason said.

"He won't make it anyway."

"We have to do what we can. There's a line shack in a mile." He snatched the whip from its socket, wrapped the lines snugly around one wrist, and slashed at the mare's hindquarters.

Bess was lathered and broken-winded when we reached the nearest gate, and by the time Freemason drew rein before a swaybacked building constructed of local stone with a patchwork roof of mud and straw, she was used up for the week, and possibly for life. A pair of smudge-bearded line riders came out to greet us with rifles, and when they recognized their employer, laid them down and helped us carry the lawyer inside. The interior was a mulch of soot and grease and tobacco and the stench of burning dung from the pit at the base of the chimney where a two-gallon coffeepot simmered on its hook, with a heavy overlay of man.

Line shacks are self-contained extensions of ranch headquarters. Because of their remoteness during heavy weather, they're as well stocked as any center of civilization. One of the riders produced medical supplies from an oilcloth pouch, cut away Cherry's blood-drenched shirt with scissors, cleaned the bubbling wound in his chest with alcohol, plucking away threads and pieces of lint with forceps, and discarded several yards of sopping red bandage in the tar bucket he and his partner used for a trash receptacle before the bleeding slowed enough to apply a patch. It was all to comfort the wounded man, like the jug whiskey they gave him from a tin cup, supporting his head with a hand while he drank; for his lungs were filling with blood and there was nothing else for it but to prop him up with pillows to slow the process and watch as he drowned on dry land.

Soon he lapsed into unconsciousness, and

at a signal from the rancher I accompanied him outside while the man who'd attended to Cherry kept an eye on him and his partner substituted a kettle for the coffeepot in the chimney and coaxed gravy from fatty chunks of mutton with a ladle. I wondered if one or both of them had been among the three hands the governor had pardoned for the murder of a fence cutter from cattle country. They'd looked more comfortable holding those rifles than they did looking after the domestic chores.

Bess had been unhitched and stood motionless in the corral apart from the linemen's mounts, head down and blowing. Freemason, athletic as slight men often are, swung himself over the top rail, seized an empty gunnysack off a nail next to the back door of the shack, and used it to rub the mare down. "I suppose we can console ourselves those road agents' informants misled them for once," he said. "I've made no new arrangements for a payroll delivery."

I said, "I see no reason to assume the virtue of truth on their behalf. Perhaps you were their target after all."

"For what purpose? They didn't rob me."

"Maybe shooting Mr. Cherry unsettled them."

"Shooting that shotgun messenger didn't

dissuade them from going ahead and robbing the Overland."

"Maybe they wanted to shoot Cherry."

"Ludicrous. Granted there's an open season on lawyers, especially with that fence-cutting bill out of committee, but they couldn't have known he'd be with me. I didn't know myself until I invited him last night."

"Who else knew?"

"Apart from whomever Cherry might have spoken to? Only my wife."

I watched him, down on one knee scrubbing rivulets of lather from a foreleg. He stopped and looked up at me through the rails. "They made a good point about that weapon you carry. I suppose English revolvers are easier to obtain in Denver."

"I wouldn't know. It's the first revolver I've ever bought. The man who sold it to me said I'd need it for protection from wolves and red Indians."

"He must have shown you how to use it. I don't believe any of the men I pay to protect my property could have produced it more quickly."

"My father told me it isn't enough just to read Scripture. One must understand it as well. It occurred to me the same would hold true for a weapon. I practiced quite a bit."

"I'm surprised you had time left to contemplate the words of our Lord. Can you hit anything with it?"

"Tins and bottles."

He rose, flicking dust from the knee of his trousers. "These bandits haven't a history of making mistakes. Perhaps I was the target, but when they shot Cherry they decided it would carry the message as well. Killing me would accomplish nothing; Colleen would appoint someone to manage the ranch in my place, because the alternative would be bankruptcy. If they frighten me off, the fence bill would lose support in Austin, and Big Cattle will continue to dominate Texas. These are not garden-variety highwaymen. Goodnight and his cronies are paying them to harass me and clear the way to claim all the grazing land for themselves."

"It seems underhanded. They've never been shy about doing battle out in the open."

"That was when they were winning, and no one in authority would oppose them. I should flatter myself that I've at least driven them to cover."

"It does help to explain why you've suffered from these robberies more than anyone," I said. "What did you make of the brand on their horses?"

"I saw no brand. I was too busy looking at their weapons."

"I got a close look when the one who disarmed us came alongside." I looked around for a stick, but good luck finding one in that country. Instead I used the toe of my shoe to trace the following symbol in the dust at my feet:

Freemason draped the sweat-soaked gunnysack over the top fence rail and leaned on it as he studied the mark, which disintegrated before our eyes in the incessant wind; in a moment, it was as if it had never existed.

"A Star of David," he said. "Do you think they're Jews?"

"If so, they'd be foolish to advertise it during robberies, given their history. I think it's more likely whoever owns the brand calls it the Double Triangle or something like that. Have you never seen it?"

"Never. I know some people with the Stock-Raisers Association; they won't let me in, but a band like this is bad business for everyone. If the brand is registered, we'll trace them."

The man we'd left with Luther Cherry opened the back door. Freemason looked a question at him, but he turned my way. "He's awake, preacher, but not for long. He wants you."

I found the lawyer propped into a half-sitting position. He'd bled through his bandages again, draining his face of all color. His lips were moving, but no sound came out. I took off my hat and bent close enough to feel his moist breath on my ear. Freemason and the man who'd come to fetch me stood at the foot of the bed. The other hand continued stirring the kettle over the fire.

"My mother was Catholic." It took Cherry twice as long to say the words as it takes to write them. "My father wouldn't have it, but she smuggled it in to me. Will you hear my confession?"

I said, "I haven't the authority to forgive you on behalf of God."

"That's all right. I don't believe a priest does either. I have some things that need saying. I don't care if you pass them on, though I'd take it a kindness if you'd spare my wife."

"I can promise that."

He spoke for several moments, drawing

whistling breaths between words. The men at the foot of the bed leaned forward, but I could barely hear him with his lips nearly touching my ear. His breath seemed to be cooling as I listened, like embers fading in a hearth. At length he stopped talking in mid-sentence. I turned my head to face him. His eyes grew soft, softer; a cloud passed between them and what lay behind. I lifted my hand and kneaded them shut.

My Bible rode in the side pocket of my coat. I took it out, but I didn't open it.

" 'The Lord is my shepherd,' " I said; " 'I shall not want. . . .' "

TWENTY-ONE

"I fail to see why you won't tell me what he told you," Freemason said. "You said yourself he didn't care so long as you kept it from his wife."

I said, "Because I can doesn't mean I should."

"But you're not a priest."

"I avoid discussions of the relative merits and deficiencies of other denominations. However, I hold the seal of the confessional to be the mainstay of the Roman Catholic Church."

"I think you're forgetting I belong to the board that employs you."

"If you want to put it on that basis, it's my Christian duty to spare you the ordeal of dismissing me. I'll submit my resignation."

"Let's not go off half-cocked, Brother. You must understand my concerns are professional as well as personal. If you know something about Cherry's behavior during the time he was representing me, it's only natural I'd press you for details."

We were in the sheepman's paneled study, where we'd retired after delivering Luther Cherry's body to the undertaking parlor that held the contract with the town council in cases of death by misadventure. Freemason had sent one of the line riders to ranch headquarters for a wagon to carry the remains. At the same time he'd sent the other man to Wichita Falls to report the incident to Captain Jordan at Texas Rangers headquarters. That day's Overland stage had come and gone, but a good man on a horse would overtake and pass it. Thought of the Overland reminded me of something I'd forgotten.

"Your interests are no more personal than Cherry's," I said. "I can tell you of a thing I saw yesterday morning at the freight office." I recounted the lawyer's argument with the clerk over the rate required to send a special delivery letter to St. Louis.

"Unpleasant, but hardly unusual," Freemason said. "The rates are outrageous, but they're the price of free enterprise. Still, everyone has the right to complain."

"Nevertheless, he paid the amount, refusing the lower rate for regular delivery

261

because it would take a few days longer. He made change from a pocketbook."

"That's what it's for. It's also called a change purse."

"Perhaps things are different in Texas, but where I come from, a man who goes to that length to corral every penny is considered parsimonious."

"They're not different. I don't use one myself, lest the men I do business with get the impression I'm hard up for cash. Cherry was cheese-paring; I admire that in someone I appoint to help handle my affairs. I fail to see why he should be condemned for it."

I looked humble, or made the effort. "It's not my place to save or condemn. I merely mentioned the episode because he was so quick to decide in favor of paying more for the sake of expediency. He said the letter was for his wife. Surely there was nothing in it so urgent it couldn't wait a few more days."

"I begin to understand you." He frowned, drumming his slim, well-kept fingers on a leaf of his towering desk. "It strikes me someone should ask the clerk in the freight office about the address on the envelope."

"He'd be violating the law if he disclosed it."

He didn't appear to be listening. "You

raise the suggestion that Cherry was the squirrel chewing holes in my wall, providing details of my business arrangements to some factotum in St. Louis, who forwarded them on to that gang of pirates."

"I wouldn't bear false witness."

"With good reason. Cherry was new to Owen. My problem predates his arrival by months."

"You told me he'd been active in the firm that represents you a long time before you retained him personally. That would put him in possession of a great deal of privileged information."

Fielo, the aged manservant, knocked and entered, carrying a tea set on a tray. His master asked him if Mrs. Freemason had returned from her errands.

"Not yet, sir. Shall I pour?"

"No. Set it down and return to your other duties. Let me know when she's back."

When the door drew shut, Freemason looked at me. "This isn't a discussion to be conducted over tea. Where do you stand on spirits?"

"I wouldn't presume. I'm told they're an ecclesiastical invention."

"Good man." He stood and used a key attached to his watch chain to unlock the hidden wall cabinet. I pretended curiosity, as if

I hadn't seen it before. "Colleen thinks the old man is a drinker on the sly," he said. "I haven't seen any evidence myself, but she's far more attuned to the domestic arrangements than I, and her attention to detail is impressive. She has a man's brain. I think that's what attracted me to her. She maintains all the books on the ranch. If something were to happen to me, I'm quite certain she could manage the place quite well on her own."

"You must trust her very much."

"A wise man told me you can trust no one or trust everyone and take the same chances. I prefer to err on the side of conservatism." He poured from the bottle of Hermitage. "I was instrumental in preventing Colleen from serving a jail sentence in Waco. She dealt cards there, which is a profession admirably suited to accounting. Between the morning she was freed and the day I proposed marriage, I had her thoroughly investigated by the Pinkertons, who confirmed everything she'd disclosed to me about her past and a number of things she neglected to mention. I'm a businessman, Brother, not a gambler. I never enter into a proposition until I've studied it from all sides and isolated the risk."

Turning from the cabinet, he held out one

of the cut-crystal glasses. When I reached for it, his free hand lashed out and enclosed my wrist in his iron grip. It was my gun hand.

"That's a pistoleer's weapon you carry," he said. "It's been well kept. In order to complete the performance, if you armed yourself at all you'd lug around some ancient cap-and-ball cannon with rust on the cylinder; but that wouldn't do if you were forced to use it. That's the flaw in any masquerade: To put it over properly one must become what one appears, rendering the exercise useless." He smiled in his neat beard. "Wouldn't you agree, Marshal?"

TWENTY-TWO

"Deputy," I corrected. "I'm not political enough for a presidential appointment. Where'd I tip my hand?"

"Where didn't you? Your choice of weapons, that history you concocted for yourself, your deportment in general. If I let go of your wrist, will you agree to keep that hand in plain sight?"

I nodded. I'd considered throwing my drink in his face to distract him while I went for the scabbard, but I hated to waste good sipping whiskey. He released his grip, poured for himself, and sat down.

"A careful way of speaking and a veil of humility can't obscure the habits of a lifetime," he said. "This morning when you came to the church door, you glanced up and down the street and scanned the rooftops before you stepped outside. I doubt you were even aware you did it. A man who's spent most of his life shut in with his mother feels no reason to take such precautions. Mind you, I suspected you before that. You have a whiff of brimstone about you. They haven't developed a soap pious enough to scrub it off."

I drank. "I was pretty certain you'd had someone go through my things. I never said I'd been shut in with my mother or even that I had one. That was all in a letter I brought with me when I came."

"It never left the parsonage, only the salient details. I told you I don't invest without investigation. My wife won't remember, but she once made reference to a former acquaintance in law enforcement who had the look of a starved wolf. That's the first impression I had of you, after disregarding the sackcloth and ashes and that collar. Excellent suggestion, that. Few people look beyond a thing so obvious."

"Thank you. It almost makes up for the heat rash."

"None of this was sufficient to leap to any conclusions, of course. Then I remembered reading of the conspicuous death of a deputy U.S. marshal of some reputation up in Montana Territory. Your choice of firearms settled the matter. Legends don't overlook such crumbs. You really ought to have left it behind."

"I hadn't time to break in a new one and keep up with my Bible studies."

"At least you're not the kind that clings to a lie in the face of all evidence. It's refreshing."

"I don't ride a horse back into a burning stable."

"I wish we'd had this conversation Sunday. It would have saved me postage to Denver. Poor Cherry was right: The rates are confiscatory."

"I ran into Fielo at the freight office. I'd guessed he was there to track down Brother Bernard."

Freemason rolled liquor on his tongue and swallowed. "Really, I thought what happened between your Judge Blackthorne and me went to rest with the Grant administration. I wouldn't have expected him to carry a grudge."

"Grudges aren't like mule packs. The bigger they are, the longer you can carry them."

"Still, he's an old political infighter. He knows when it's time to cut your losses and get back to business."

"A lot of lawyers lost their case because they thought they could predict him." My mouth was dry, but I resisted raising my glass because my hand might shake. I was close to an explanation of why I was in Texas.

"Just what is he after? In ten years I've done nothing that would place me in his power. Or is it your mission to adjust that situation? I believe you said something a few moments ago about bearing false witness."

I shot from the hip. "Nothing like that. The law's his lasso. He'll take a couple of dallies on it, but he won't break it. Some new evidence has come to light to make that old grudge a little easier to carry."

Fielo knocked, came in at his master's invitation, and reported that Mrs. Freemason had returned. Freemason nodded and dismissed him. When we were alone again, the rancher sat back for the first time and steepled his hands. I knew then I'd misfired.

"No new evidence can reverse a presidential pardon," he said. "Blackthorne didn't tell you anything about our history. I'd thought you were remarkably circumspect for a man of action. What's your real purpose? I can have you locked up as an impostor, on suspicion of your intentions. With all this banditry about, and when information comes back from Denver casting doubt on the existence of a preacher named Sebastian, no one will question your incarceration for weeks."

"I've been in jail before." I was making time to think. Whatever was in the Judge's mind, it would collapse under its own weight while I was behind bars, and with no way to get in touch with him, I'd be stuck counting stones in the walls while the Blue Bandannas were free to hare around shooting cowhands and shotgun messengers and generally breaking the peace. I drank, no tremors, and set aside my glass. "Until I came here, I didn't even know you and Blackthorne had a history. The first time I saw your name was when I read it on your telegram inviting Brother Bernard to serve as pastor. I was sent to investigate the panhandle robberies."

"That's a tale. Every one of them took place outside his jurisdiction."

"Strictly speaking, his jurisdiction covers all crimes against the United States. Two of the robberies involved the mail. Also he's concerned that left to its own devices this band will eventually expand their depredations to Montana Territory. He'd rather fight them on the High Plains than in Virginia City."

"He said that?"

"He did."

"Did you believe him?"

"I wasn't required to."

"I don't believe you."

"Let's talk about something else, then. For what crime were you pardoned by President Grant?"

He checked that without blinking. "You said you knew nothing about my connection with Blackthorne until you came here. Who told you?"

I was busy saying nothing when Colleen Freemason entered without knocking. Clearly she'd been listening outside the door. "I told him, Richard."

She was dressed fetchingly in a straw hat with a curled brim and feathers, a trim tweed suit over a plain shirtwaist, black-and-ivory patent-leather pumps, and black felt gloves with ivory buttons. Her cheeks were flushed from the wind. As she was naturally high-colored, she might have stepped out of a Renaissance painting and come there by way of a Victorian dress shop. She was staring at me; accusingly or not, I could never tell.

"Indeed," Freemason said. "The past becomes the present. That wasn't our arrangement."

"Nothing's changed. I made the same error you did. I assumed he was here to try to snare you in some way. From what I just overheard, you told him more than I did."

I turned my attention from her, which was always a chore. "Since you did, you might as well tell me the rest. I've been floundering in the dark since before I left Helena."

Freemason frowned, then pulled his hands apart and placed them on the arms of his chair. His mouth opened; Colleen stepped close and placed a gloved hand on his shoulder.

"The past is not the present." She was still looking at me. "We've made our home here. We've obeyed the law, and Richard has assisted it. You're the one who's sailing under false colors. We owe you nothing."

"A pretty speech," said her husband. "I'd be more impressed if you'd *told* me his colors were false. Have you taken up where you left off?"

She snatched away her hand as if he'd bitten it.

I anted in. "She made it clear the last time we spoke in this room there'd be none of that. I swore my business here had nothing to do with you and Blackthorne and asked her to keep the secret. Too many people knew already, and there was no telling what someone else might guess if your attitude toward me was any different from what was expected between a church director and his parson. Not wanting to see a man murdered in the course of his work and having serious feelings for him aren't the same thing."

"We both have secrets, Richard. We agreed we weren't each other's confessor."

"A fine match." He swirled the contents of his glass, then tossed them back like any hand fresh off the trail. Then he got up to refill.

"Pour me one as well." Colleen stripped off her gloves and drew the pin from her hat.

"I keep coming back to why those bandits were waiting for us," I said when we were all seated. "Until now, they've made no mistakes. Their sources have been too good."

Freemason still looked sour, and it had only a little to do with what had happened near his ranch. "Everyone puts a foot wrong sometimes. I married a woman I can't trust."

"I don't care. You're forgetting I'm not really a minister. One mistake is possible, but this was also the first time they've struck this close to Owen. Their avoiding it is what brought me here in the first place. They must have had a compelling reason to break that cardinal rule. Whenever something like that happens, I ask myself what recent change might have brought it about."

"That would be you." Colleen, informed of the day's events, sat upright in a chintz-covered chair, the only remotely feminine object in the room and obviously kept for her use. She held her glass at bodice level with the surface of the liquid as flat as a sheltered pond. "You're Owen's newest resident."

"Just barely. Luther Cherry arrived just before me."

"You keep harping on Cherry," Freemason said. "He's dead."

"Another mistake. He made a grab for his briefcase when it slid off his lap. He was under the gun at the time, and when you have someone in that position the shooter's nerves are right up there on top. Shooting him was a natural reaction on the part of the man with the Spencer."

"Also disastrous, if you insist on believing that Cherry was their Trojan horse. That makes three mistakes. What are the odds of that happening, given their record so far?"

"Colleen's the cardplayer," I said.

She shook her head and sipped. "I'd fold rather than bet against them. It was no accident."

I said, "I think it was. Killing him, I mean.

Everything else was planned. They weren't expecting a payroll wagon. That was just an excuse. Cherry was just settling in, and Freemason hadn't made it a secret he suspected he had a traitor in his employ. What better way to raise their man inside above suspicion than to shoot him during an attempted robbery, right in front of his employer?"

"By God." Freemason flushed deep copper, his glass hovering beneath his chin. "By God."

"The man I'll call Spencer meant to wing him," I went on, "but that's not an exact science when you're on horseback and your target's in motion. Either his aim was off or Cherry moved in the wrong direction. The bullet pierced a lung instead of just an arm."

The sheepman remembered his drink and took a long draught. "Are frontier brigands capable of such Machiavellian measures?"

"The organized ones are," I said. "We're up against a bigger operation than any of us thought. If I'm right about that special delivery letter Cherry sent to St. Louis, it means he had a contact there who forwarded privileged information on to whoever the Blue Bandannas report to in this area. Someone's out to break you, and he's going to a hell of a lot of expense to do it."

"The cattle trade," he said. "That fence-cutting bill has them scared. If they manage to destroy me, no one will ever enforce it, and there will be no sheep rancher safe in the state of Texas."

I emptied my glass and set it down. "Cattlemen are too busy running their own spreads to act in concert. Maybe they've appointed someone, but whoever's behind the robberies has nothing else on his plate to distract him."

"I'll trace that letter Cherry made so much fuss about."

"You can do that. Chances are he sent it to someone at the legal firm you got him from, who can claim it was just some unfinished business; certainly he'll have destroyed the evidence, and all we'll have is Cherry's lie that he was writing his wife."

"Maybe his wife is the go-between."

Both of us looked at Colleen, whose chin elevated an inch in defense of her theory.

"She isn't," I said.

"How do you know?" she asked.

"Because when he confessed to conspiring against Freemason, he asked me to say nothing of it to her."

TWENTY-THREE

Freemason toyed with his glass. "Why didn't you tell me what he said the first time I asked? What was the point of pretending to speculate he died as a result of his own manipulations?"

"That part was speculation," I said. "He didn't live long enough to get around to it. As for the rest, I wasn't sure he was alone. I'm still not, but based on this conversation I'm reasonably satisfied it isn't your wife."

Colleen appeared unmoved; but so does the outside of a volcano. "What did I say to convince you I'm not?"

"Nothing. If you had, you'd still be under suspicion. It's never easy to tell when you're bluffing, but the higher the stakes, the harder you push a pair of deuces. You didn't say a word when your husband said he couldn't trust you. If ever there was a time for a traitor to prove herself loyal, that was it."

"God, but you're a bastard."

"I've worked for Blackthorne a long time. Some of it was bound to rub off." A clock outside the door chimed the hour; we'd been locked up most of the day. I looked at Freemason. "You'll see to Cherry's arrangements, I suppose. No doubt his wife will want to bury him in St. Louis."

"I ought to throw his carcass into the creek, but I've become a respectable man. I'll play the generous benefactor. The damage is done; nothing can be gained by blackening his memory. And what will you be about meanwhile?"

"Sunday is Easter. I've a sermon to prepare." I rose. Two pairs of eyes followed me.

Freemason said, "You intend to continue as Brother Bernard? Why? Without Cherry, the Bandannas have no hole card. The first time they act on their own they'll blunder into the hands of the Rangers as like as not."

"I said I'm not sure he was alone. In any case my orders are to break them up or bring them to justice. Also the church needs a pastor."

"Where will you start?" he asked.

"Matthew, twenty-six."

"You're trying my patience, Deputy."

"Brother," I said. "Let's not slip into any bad habits. I'm going to start by tracing that star brand. They've got as good an eye for horseflesh as any outlaw gang. The trader who sold seven premium mounts at a crack will remember who he sold them to."

He said, "The brand might not be registered. Smaller ranches crop up all the time. The ranchers are too busy getting established to bother right away, and the registrars can't keep up with the rest."

"You don't get animals like that from a start-up outfit. Someone had time to breed them. The brand has to be on file somewhere."

"Still, that's a lot of legwork for one man."

"If you're trying to find out how I operate, you're wasting my time as well as yours."

He flushed again. "You don't care who you insult, do you?"

Colleen said, "He has rules about which questions to answer honestly when he's playing a role, Richard. He likes to keep his lies in a separate pile, and he doesn't trust anyone."

I shook my head. "You can trust everyone and be betrayed, or no one and betray yourself. My policy is to shoot straight down the middle."

"Even so," Freemason said. "Not trusting is a quality a man can do worse than to acquire."

The old Mexican came in after knocking, hesitated when he saw we were all standing, and spoke in a low tone to Freemason, who bent his head to listen. "Tell him to come in."

Fielo ghosted out, leaving the door open for the visitor. Captain Jordan of the Texas Rangers stood taller than he sat, despite bowed legs and a slight shoulder stoop. He wore what appeared to be the same faded blue flannel shirt, its pockets stuffed with smoking material, with leather-reinforced riding trousers stuffed into the tops of tall stovepipe boots, long-roweled Mexican spurs jingling behind the heels. He took off his pinch hat, revealing a bald crown cream-colored to the line where the hat ended and his tan began. He smelled of the sweat of horse and man. The steel-shot eyes looked tired and a stubble had sprouted on his chin, as white as his handlebars.

He introduced himself, grasped the sheepman's hand, and nodded to Colleen. When Freemason presented me, the Ranger showed no recognition. His grip would be the last thing about him to give out.

"What luck?" Freemason asked.

"Same as at White Horse," Jordan said. "Tracks turned into the creek and got lost in the tangle from the last herd that crossed. They know this country, all right. Can't figure out what made them steer so wide of it before this."

"Brother Bernard has a theory about that," began Freemason, only to abandon the rest at a look from me.

"I'm always open to spiritual guidance." Jordan nailed me with his gaze.

I smiled an apology. "That's the only kind I can offer. I just suggested that poor Mr. Cherry may have been the reason the gang singled us out."

"Any special reason, or does God speak just to you?"

It was an experience new to me, that moment: Two men working overtime to keep a third from knowing the full truth about one of them while the third pretended not to know it already. The frontier was no longer the simple place it used to be.

I told him of the lawyer's last words, and my thought that he'd engineered his own wounding in order to lift suspicion from himself. Jordan took it all in without comment. Colleen excused herself as a nonwitness and left us. The captain declined a drink, stuffed and lit his pipe, and gave us a detailed account of his quest beginning with the message Freemason had sent him in

Wichita Falls by way of the rider from the ranch: He and his small command had traded their lathered mounts for fresh ones Freemason had made available for them at the line shack and followed the trail to extinction. He'd left his men to rest in town while he came to the house to report and gather information.

"What encouragement can you offer that I won't end up fighting this band over my last dollar?" asked the rancher.

"Not knowing how many you got, I can't answer. If the brother's right, a cockeyed scheme like that is a sign they're losing their smarts. However, I ain't what you might call a religious man. The evidence of things unseen don't hold up in San Antonio."

"What's the reward on these fellows' capture or death?"

"Five hundred a head."

"I'll add a hundred each, and see if I can get the Stock-Raisers Association to double it."

"That ought to make things right lively. If I had a blue bandanna I'd burn it." Jordan stood and offered his hand. "I'd like to ask the brother a couple of questions, just us. He's the one Cherry talked to. He might remember a thing or two more in a place where he's comfortable."

"You don't have to ask my permission, Captain. That's up to Brother Bernard."

"I'm afraid I can't tell you anything I haven't, Captain."

His lips parted to let something out, but I jigged my eyes right and left, hoping he wasn't an unsubtle man. He drew a breath and stirred his handlebars on the exhale. "Well, if you can't take a preacher at his word, who can you? It's getting late and I don't trust that stage trail. I'll spread my roll outside town and start back at first light. This trail won't get no warmer."

"I've got spare rooms gathering dust," Freemason said. "I'd consider it a favor if you'd put up here. Mrs. Freemason and I don't get many visitors. Pariahs, don't you know, under the veneer of respect."

"I'll remember you asked next time. Just now I got men getting set to stretch out on bare panhandle. It wouldn't set right with them to know I spent the night on feathers."

We left that house. At the bottom of the long flight of steps Jordan and I shook hands. "The parsonage behind the church," I said. "After dark. I'll leave the back door off the latch."

He didn't even nod, although I could feel the heat of curiosity glowing deep in those

burnished eyes. We turned in opposite directions. As I did so I caught a glimpse of a
curtain stirring in an upstairs window of
the mansion. When she'd moved in, Colleen
would have been sure to secure herself a
room with the best view of the town.

The sun was long gone when someone
tapped at the back door of the parsonage.
I'd moved the lamp in the little sitting room
to a spot where it wouldn't outline the
opening and closed and latched the door
behind him quickly. The sacking someone
had put up to serve for curtains masked the
windows.

"I don't see the need," Jordan said when
we were seated. I'd given him the rocking
chair, filled two tin cups from the bottle I'd
brought from Helena, and drawn the
straightback close so we could talk quietly.
There didn't have to be professional spies;
the Fielos and Mrs. McIlvaines of the world
have soft soles and long ears. "I thought I
did a fair job of explaining the palaver."

"I've got my reasons," I said. "They don't
have to make sense to anyone but me."

He didn't pursue the point, and my respect for him went up another healthy
notch. He tipped his hat as far back as only
a Texan can without it falling off. "I'd as lief

wrestle bobwire in the dark as have another meet like that one at Freemason's. Just who knows what?"

"His wife and I have a history. She kept her mouth shut, but he figured it out based on some things she'd told him in the past. Neither of them knows you and I have met before. I'd like to keep it that way for a while. People let down their guard when they think one man is all they have to worry about."

"I knowed something was in the wind when you gave me the evil eye there at the finish. First Cherry, now his boss? How big is this bunch?"

"I don't know, but Cherry wasn't in it."

He drank from his cup, his eyes fixed on mine above the rim. "Why would a man lie his way into hell with his last breath? And how do you know he did?"

"I don't. He confessed, but not to informing on Freemason's plans. He wanted me to know he'd strayed once from his marriage. It happened just the one time, he said, back in St. Louis, but he didn't want to die with it on his conscience. He asked me not to tell his wife. I think what happened had something to do with why he accepted Freemason's invitation to set up shop here in Texas.

"He was talking to the collar," I went on. "I'll probably draw another month in purgatory for it."

"That was the shebang? He jumped the traces?"

"If there was anything else he didn't last long enough to share it. In that situation you lead with the sin that's most on your mind."

"So why did you tell Freemason — Oh." The dawn appeared to break. He nodded. "That's why I came in the back way. How sure are you?"

"Not enough to take any sort of action. Subtracting Cherry, it's the only explanation for what happened out on the road, but I can't take that to Helena. Anyway, you can see why I didn't want anyone to think I had the chance to pass on what I knew to the Rangers. I have to be the lightning rod."

"A lightning rod can take a lot of hits. With a man, all it takes is one."

"I've been struck before."

He shook his leonine head. "I got to tell you, this is one game of poker where you're safer to share your cards."

"The deck's passed through too many hands as it is." I lifted my cup, but didn't drink. I tapped a finger on the rim and lowered it. "I've a strong hunch you can hold a secret till it sprouts leaves, but my hunches don't always turn out. It has to stop somewhere. I can't even trust my friends with what I plan to do next."

"Lone wolves are easier to kill. Just so you know."

"That doesn't mean it's easy. But if it happens, it means I figured right. The rest will be up to you."

He got out his pipe, leaving the makings in his pocket. He slid the stem along his lower lip, watching me through the thickets of creases that surrounded his eyes. "I don't mind dying while I'm moving forward. I'd sure as hell hate it while I'm going the other direction. They don't pay me enough to do it standing still. What do they pay you up there?"

"Free burial, same as you. Did you bring anything for me?"

"Thought you'd ask. Since I was fixing to be in the neighborhood I took it along." He gave me a thick fold of yellow paper from the flap pocket where he kept his tobacco pouch.

I unfolded it. It was a garble of unrelated words consuming several pages of Western Union scrip, signed HAB. Harlan A. Blackthorne's personal code was more complex than the one I'd worked out with Jordan, but it was a lot less chatty in appearance; anyone who saw it would know immediately it contained confidential information. I was relieved to see it was addressed to the Rangers station and not Bernard Sebastian.

"Anything for me?" Jordan asked.

"I don't know yet. It takes time to work out. I'll get word to you if there is."

"What you fixing to do now, fort up here and wait?"

"I'd just as soon post my plans on the church bulletin board. The biggest day in the Christian year is coming up; I expect a full house Sunday, and I have to get ready for it."

"I was you, I'd sling a skillet around my neck front and back. So far the Lord God Jesus is the only one ever clumb back up out of the grave come Easter."

"Well, I died up north and here I sit. Maybe He's got another miracle for me in His pocket."

TWENTY-FOUR

The lamp was guttering when I left off translating the Judge's response to my question about Freemason and turned in. I finished in the morning, but by then I'd already learned enough to piece together the rest. The old bastard behind the bench had been wise to wait until I was a thousand miles away before he opened Pandora's box.

I worked on my Easter sermon over coffee, ate noon dinner at the Pan Handle, where Charlie Sweet was too busy waiting tables to exchange more than a couple of friendly words, and made my first two missionary stops, to the Alamo and the Old Granada saloons, where the cowhands and the sheep hands did their respective drinking.

In the Alamo the bartender, a stove-up old waddie with a rolling limp and a permanent squint, gave me a look intended for a natural enemy, and my collar made the customers nervous, anticipating a weekday sermon, but I put them all back on their heels by buying drinks for the men I stood with at the bar while ordering well water for myself. On the second round I moved my glass, leaving a wet ring on the glossy cherrywood, and traced a pair of intersecting triangles with my finger. I asked the men at my right and left if they'd seen a brand that looked like it. Each man looked closely, traded his position with the others to give them a view, and shook his head. The bartender finished drawing a beer, came over, and wiped away the symbol with his rag, muttering something that sounded like Hebrew. That threw me a little.

I drew the same blank at the Old Granada, where a pastoral engraving of a bearded shepherd and his flock hung above the bottles of busthead. Two of the sheep hands there saw the mark's resemblance to the Star of David, but no one had seen it in the flesh.

By then the local meeting place of the Texas Stock-Raisers Association, which occupied the second floor of the Elks Lodge, had opened its doors for dinner. The gatekeeper, a Prussian in a cutthroat collar with a straight back and military whiskers, sat me on a hard bench inside the entryway and kept me waiting for a half hour while he checked in diners, then as the flow ebbed sent a waiter to the little club library for a brand book. I spread it open on my knees, turned page after page of crudely drawn insignia, and found exactly what I'd expected: Nothing. For whatever reason — possibly one as harmless as its owner hadn't registered in time to make that year's record — the spread where the bandits' horses were raised didn't appear to exist in the eyes of the ranching establishment. That left me as heavy as ever on suspicion but as light as usual on evidence.

The First Unitarian was packed for the second Sunday in a row, which I attributed more to the holiness of the day than to my skills as a spellbinder, although I flattered myself that I hadn't driven anyone into the arms of the Methodists. Richard and Colleen Freemason were in their customary pew up front; a brass plate on the end of the backrest bore witness to their contribution in its construction, as did the others celebrating other donors, but in their case the Masonic compass and square took the place of a name. I saw other familiar faces as well as some new ones among the worshippers standing in back. The lay volunteer circulating the collection plate had to dump his load in the old Wells, Fargo box on the platform behind the pulpit and go back for seconds. There was a new coat of paint there and roof repairs. I never was in a house of God that wasn't stumping for a new roof: Church shingles take a double beating, from rain above and prayers below.

I'd gone through the portfolio of sermons Eldred Griffin had placed in my charge and made a risky choice. The text rejected the common view of Judas' betrayal of Jesus as villainy, transforming him into a kind of flawed, tragic hero, who when he realized the enormity of his transgression had chosen to take his own life rather than to confess and repent, thus sentencing himself to an eternity in hell without parole. It fell short of expiating his guilt, but it hinted at personal redemption. As originally written, the sermon bordered on heresy; I was next to certain that Griffin had composed it after his own fall from grace, with no intention of ever reading it in public, and as such it required editing to avoid having myself nailed to the sorry crooked wooden sticks that West Texas had to offer in the way of a cross. I laid in the conventional condemnation of Iscariot and powdered it lightly with the defrocked priest's mercy, leavening out the sardonic quality with which it was drenched.

I don't know why I made the selection, except I was already out on a limb holding an anvil and an ounce this way or that didn't matter. Whatever happened, I'd presided over my last service in Owen.

There was a short silence after I finished, but no murmurs, and when I called for "Lead, Kindly Light," everyone in the congregation joined in.

"A bold piece." Freemason took my hand at the door. He looked puzzled. "Do you always fly this close to the flame?"

"The man who wrote it showed me how close is too close." There was now no reason to pretend authorship.

"You must tell me about him sometime."

"He wouldn't like it. He's bent on disappearance."

"Fugitive?"

"Yes, I think that describes him."

We were speaking low, but he leaned in close and dropped his voice almost to a whisper. "What luck tracing that brand?"

"It's not in the book, and none of the ranch hands I talked to remember seeing it."

"It must be a pirate outfit. They comb other spreads for mares with foals too young for branding, pare the mares' hooves to the quick so they can't wander far, and when the foals are ready to wean they rustle them and burn their own mark. It's as if the animals never existed. A fully grown unbranded horse invites investigation, but registering the brand involves answering too many questions. No one knows just how many such ranches exist. It's an impossible quest."

"Those are the ones I usually get."

"You're not dissuaded?"

I looked at him, but he was a hard man to read. "Do you want me to be?"

"I think it's too much for one man. Your death would weigh heavily on my conscience."

"Jordan and his Rangers are working on that brand, but they're spread thin themselves. I'm thinking of asking Judge Blackthorne to lean on the governor to put every available company on the job."

"That's wise, but why go so far around the barn? I'm sure I can persuade Ireland to see reason. That brand is the first thing we've found that can provide a link to the man responsible for these raids."

"With you applying pressure from below and Blackthorne applying it from above, I don't see how he can refuse the accommodation."

"At least let me send a rider to Wichita Falls with your message. The Overland proceeds at its own pace."

"I'll use both, in case one or the other is waylaid."

We regarded each other. It was the biggest time-waster anyone could imagine, even on a Sunday: Two men talking circles around the thing they both knew.

Colleen interrupted the game. In honor of the day she wore a purple velvet dress with a hat to match, trailing a broad yellow ribbon down her back to her waist. In one kid glove she clutched a closed parasol, yellow with purple trim. "Once again, Richard, you're holding up the line." She offered me her free hand. "Another intriguing sermon. A bit cosmopolitan for Owen, don't you think? The people around here prefer their badmen painted in black with thick strokes."

I met her blue gaze, harder than Jordan's, more opaque than Freemason's. "I like purple."

She smiled. "What a pretty compliment."

They moved on. The friendly freight office clerk shook my hand, wrenching me from my reflections. His face was troubled. "I was raised to love Jesus and hate Judas. Now I don't know what to think."

"Hate is the devil's seed," I said. That seemed to lift his spirits.

My reviews were mixed; I could tell by the silences as well as by the remarks. The man who had snored through most of my first services wrung my palm and gave me high marks for preaching against sin; plainly he'd awakened just in time to join the exodus for the door. Some people who'd stopped to greet me last Sunday swept on past the line without pausing. I didn't expect them back even if I thought I'd be back myself. I made mental note of everything to report to Griffin, who might be interested to know the reaction, even though I was sure it wouldn't surprise him.

I felt an indifference bordering on atheism. It had been important that my debut was positive enough to assure me some time in the community. Whether I left it with a sour taste in its mouth signified nothing. One way or the other, my time in Owen was growing short.

For a time after the last carriage creaked away, I stood at the pulpit pretending to make corrections in the margins of my notes while Mrs. McIlvaine's broom swished relentlessly in the corners. My pencil drew meaningless coils on the foolscap, unconsciously imitating the patterns of dust turning in the shortening shafts of sunlight coming through the windows. They circled patiently, killing time as they waited for the bristles to stop moving so they could settle. It seemed God's plan that there should be dust, and that any attempt to banish it from His place on earth was doomed from the start; but housekeepers, too, have a patron saint, so their efforts carry some kind of endorsement. Everyone seemed to have one, except lawmen posing as ministers of the faith. I knew, because I'd looked it up. Nomads of the desert have one, so do nurses and the sick, innkeepers, storytellers, the desperate, fishermen, even thieves. Impostors alone are without representation. What did it matter what miracles you accomplished for the United States District Court if they condemned you in the court of heaven?

The assignment had gotten under my skin worse than all the others. I'd flogged whiskey and mucked out stalls for cover, been a Cheyenne slave and shared a cell with a matricide — rotten work, but you can scrub off the stink of sour mash, recover from prison food, and a good laundress can boil the manure stains out of your clothes. In time, exposure to other peoples and their ways can even restore your belief in the basic humanity of every race. Everything was reversible, except Moses and Ezekiel and Ruth and Solomon and Matthew. Once they burrowed under your skin they were there to stay, like the heads of chiggers. There wasn't a miserable deed or an act of charity in the Good Book that didn't resemble something I'd witnessed and had sometimes been part of. The words of those drifters and cobblers and drones and harlots and the odd bearded king were more accurate than *The Farmer's Almanack*.

At length the swishing stopped, a door thudded into its frame, and I was alone. Still I didn't stir from the pulpit, although I folded my pages and poked them into my breast pocket near the revolver in its rig. I stood gazing at the empty pews, feeling the reflected warmth from the squares of daylight creeping toward the east windows, smelling candle wax and walnut stain and the eternal dust, the dust of the Eternal, the presence of the Lord in every restless grain, searching for a place to lay His head and not finding it for more than a moment.

I brought up the Bible from its shelf beneath the lectern, rested it on its loose spine, and let go. It fell open to Second Kings, chapter twenty:

In those days was Hezekiah sick unto death. And the prophet Isaiah the son of Amoz came to him, and said unto him, Thus saith the Lord, Set thine house in order; for thou shalt die, and not live.

I found that unsatisfactory. I was riffling through the pages for something more encouraging when a window flew apart and I fell over backward with what felt like the entire church resting on my chest.

Twenty-Five

I'd had my fill of being shot at, whether I was part of the plan or not. When I realized I hadn't been hit, that when the bullet came through the window I'd gripped the edges of the pulpit from instinct and brought it down with me, landing on my chest and knocking out my wind, I got mad and shoved it off with strength I didn't have under ordinary circumstances. The Deane-Adams was in my hand now and I made my way on knees and elbows to the broken pane, wheezing as I did so; I couldn't seem to take in enough air to satisfy my need. It was like swimming in deep water without having gulped in enough oxygen first.

I raised my head just high enough to see out, resting the barrel of the revolver on the sill, strewn with glass fragments and shards of molding. Out in the street the driver of a wagon loaded with furniture was straining at the lines, trying to keep his brace of walleyed, pawing grays from plunging, and townsmen were leaning out through doors and around the sides of porch posts, looking toward the church or turning their heads toward the rooftops across the street. That meant a rifle or carbine, discharging loudly enough in the open air to alert the town. When the gawkers ventured out from cover and started churchward, I knew the shooter was long gone. I stood.

Too fast. A swarm of bats flew off their perches inside my head, blocking out the light. I fell into the middle of them.

The crack in the plaster ceiling looked familiar. The first time I'd seen it I thought it looked like the bad map I'd followed into Murfreesboro with General Rosecrans. It was directly above the iron-framed bed in the parsonage.

Something tinkled. I thought of pieces of glass falling out of the window frame in the church and reached for my suspender scabbard, but I wasn't wearing it, or a shirt. I lay stripped to my waist on the top sheet. I took a tentative breath, then a deeper one. The air was as sweet as sugar. I gulped in a bellyful and let it out in a whoosh.

"It's amazing, is it not, how grateful one can be for the things he takes for granted, once he's been deprived of them? But then I shouldn't have to tell a minister that."

I recognized the voice without knowing why. I turned my head and watched a man with a spray of beard to the third button of his waistcoat returning instruments to his case. That was the tinkling I'd heard, and I knew him now for Dr. Littlejohn, one of the town's practitioners and a man who'd approved of both my sermons at the church door. He was sitting in the straightback from the sitting room, wearing a Masonic medal on his watch chain. He had the same insignia in brass on the latch of his black leather bag. I wondered if he was a creature of Freemason's or just a member of the brotherhood.

I used my tongue to clear the cobwebs from my mouth. "I had a horse squatting on my chest." My voice still sounded like cornhusks rustling.

"I thought at first you had a collapsed lung, but by the time I had your shirt off you'd begun to breathe normally, so it must have been temporary paralysis brought on by physical trauma. Pulpits are meant to stand behind, not used as counterpanes. You blacked out because you weren't taking in enough oxygen to feed your brain cells. I was afraid I'd have to crack your chest and insert a rubber tube to draw off the pressure."

"Have you ever done that?"

"No. I confess I was a little disappointed not to have the opportunity."

"Are you always this honest with your patients?"

"My practice would be more successful if I weren't. You're rather an unusual man in your profession yourself."

"Men of God have been shot at before."

"Not many react in kind or so quickly. That piece of furniture that fell on you is solid hickory. Most men would still be struggling to get out from under it when help arrived. You tossed it aside like a match and threw down on the enemy."

I turned my head the other way, and was relieved to see the Deane-Adams on the nightstand. "It's the second time in a week I had a bullet pass close to me. You get mad."

"Wrath isn't necessarily a sin. In this case it may have saved your life. You could have suffocated under the constriction."

"Who — ?"

"Mrs. Freemason. She was on her way here for a visit when the shot rang out. She found you passed out on the floor and sent for me. By the time I got here, she'd recruited volunteers to carry you in here. I told her that was unwise; for all she knew, you had a broken back, and moving you might have been fatal. She said she knew a broken back when she saw one. How do you suppose she knew that?" He sat back with the bag on his lap, his hands resting on his thighs.

"She's a woman of many parts. Where is she?"

"In your sitting room. She's been waiting twenty minutes. I told her she should go home, but she demurred."

"Demurred."

He frowned in his impressive whiskers. "I agree the term seems inadequate. However, she has a way of slamming the door soundly on an argument with the air of someone declining an invitation to badminton."

"She's a well-bred jenny. What do I owe you?"

"I have my soul to consider. A day and a night in that bed will suffice, for what my counsel is worth. I've an idea you're a mule from the same paddock."

"I always heard the Masons were honest men."

He fingered the engraving on his bag. "The clergy hasn't always been so charitable toward the order. When Father Cress sees me coming he crosses himself as if I were the Prince of Lies in person."

"Is it true your founders claimed to have removed the body of Christ from its tomb?"

"That's a canard," he said, reddening. "Catholic fanatics have been repeating it since before the Inquisition. We are a benevolent foundation, and as such represent competition with the Church. There's the source of these centuries of black blood."

The emotion in his voice assured me of his affiliation. I said I'd pray for him.

His color paled to normal. He rose, rested his bag on the chair, and drew the blanket up from the foot of the bed to cover me to the collarbone. "The proprieties, don't you know. I'll send her in now, but she can't stay long. I want to check your ribs while you're conscious to make sure they're not cracked and pinching. I'll bind them if they are. You bled a bit through the knees of your trousers, probably from lacerations when you were crawling through broken glass. They'll need cleaning and sticking plaster."

"I can see to that, and the ribs. This isn't the first spill I've taken."

"I didn't realize preaching the gospel was so dangerous."

I'd forgotten myself. The brain is slowest to recover when you've stepped back from the stony edge. "I was an awkward child."

"All the same," he said after a tense moment, "I'll stay and complete the examination. We can't have you surviving an attempt on your life only to pierce a lung with the end of a broken rib."

"You haven't asked why I was shot at."

"I assumed it was because of the subject of your sermon this morning. Judas is somewhat less popular in the State of Texas than General Santa Anna."

That was a bald lie, the assumption part, and he could see I knew it, but I didn't press the point. If there's a man who can keep a secret as well as a minister, he has *Doctor* in front of his name. Nevertheless, here was one more recruit to the side of the doubters. In a little while, that shot would be heard throughout the panhandle. My sheep's clothing was falling away in great bloody patches.

She came in with none of the hesitation of a respectable woman entering a man's bedroom, as if she were walking into her own. I'd seen her do that, with me following, but that wasn't going to happen ever again. She had on the velvet dress she'd worn to church, without the hat. The sunlight coming in through the front windows made a copper-colored aura around her pinned-up hair. Black as it comes, there is always red in it.

I gathered myself into a sitting position. I was careful about it, but a phantom blow struck my chest as if the pulpit had taken a second crack at me. I leaned back against the bedstead, breathing with my mouth open. No pinches, at least, so maybe no cracked ribs. I'd cracked my share, all right, falling off horses and grappling with unarmed fugitives, which made me something of an expert.

"Nasty bruise," she said, glancing at my chest.

"Call it divine retribution. It could've been worse. A Spencer packs a hell of a wallop inside its range."

"You saw it?"

"I didn't have to. I was expecting it."

"Evidently."

I lifted a hand and let it drop to the blanket. "I thought it would happen out in the open. I fell into the sanctuary trap. That isn't a mistake I'd have made a few weeks ago. When the disguise assumes you, it's time to take it off and pin the badge back on."

"You never pin it on."

"That's what I was saying. That collar cuts

307

off the blood flow to the brain. My instincts of self-preservation went with it."

She transferred the doctor's bag to the floor, inspected the seat of the chair for dust, and sat, resting her reticule in her lap. "I was certain you were dead."

"I disappoint a lot of people."

"I'm the one who sent for the doctor."

"There wasn't any reason not to, once you saw I hadn't been shot."

"I'm many things, Page, but a murderess isn't one of them."

I let that blow in the damn Texas wind. "What were you coming to see me about?"

"You're welcome. I should have known you wouldn't fall all over yourself with gratitude."

"Thanks. What were you coming to see me about?"

"I came to warn you."

"You came late."

"I was late finding out. You're behaving as if you wished it were anyone else."

"It wouldn't be the first time, when it was you."

"We weren't always enemies, you know."

I said nothing, watching her.

She shook her head infinitesimally. "Don't pretend. You never did know when I was bluffing."

The reticule was purple trimmed with yellow to match the rest of her kit. Colleen Bower was capable of letting her house burn down around her while she selected just the right ensemble for flight. She untied the bag and brought out a small rectangular envelope with the initials *C.B.* embossed in one corner; the *B* standing for either Bower or Baronet, her most recent married name but one. She wasn't the kind to let a powerful man like Freemason slap his brand on her.

The word *brand* echoed in my head, for any number of reasons. It turned a lingering trace of cold fire, like incendiaries on Independence Day. My mind was still moving at a dead walk.

I took the envelope from her gloved hand. "Your hole card?"

"A note. I couldn't be sure I'd find you in. God alone knows where a minister goes after the last 'Amen.' "

I lifted the flap, took out the matching letterhead, and snapped it open:

You're in greater danger than you know.

It was unsigned, but I knew her hand. I ran my thumb over the indentations the pen had made in the soft rag stock. There was a pale spot in the lower loop of the *d,* where the ink had run out and she'd paused to re-dip. She couldn't have manufactured it in my sitting room, and twenty minutes weren't enough to make the round trip to her house and back. A woman of her standing in the community couldn't afford to carry around a pot of ink and risk a stain on her handbag. A pencil and coarse paper were the only writing paraphernalia in the parsonage.

She was telling the truth. I waited for the earth to slip off its axis, but it went on creaking around, one miracle at a time.

I stuck the note back in its envelope and returned it. In that moment I knew my brain had been trying to tell me something. "I saw the brand on Freemason's buggy horse," I said.

"He puts it on everything. He doesn't belong, but he's obsessed with it because of his name. He wouldn't have the patience to go through initiation."

Her husband's brand was a stylized version of the Masonic compass and square:

"Hand me that bag." I pointed to the doctor's case on the floor.

She hesitated, then complied. I rooted among the brown bottles and wicked-looking instruments inside, found a grease pencil, and made alterations on the fraternal symbol etched on the latch, drawing two lines only:

TWENTY-SIX

"A Star of David?" she said.

"Just a star. This one never had anything to do with religion."

"Is that the brand you saw on the bandits' horses?"

"One horse, but I've been all through that with Freemason. You can always tell when a string was raised under the same conditions. It only takes twenty seconds with a running iron to change two intersecting *V*'s into a star. Freemason was smart enough not to send the Blue Bandannas out marauding on horses wearing a mark from his spread, but he's a sheepman. He underestimated a cowboy's eye."

"Not by much, in this case."

"I haven't swung a lariat since you were in swaddles, but it's true I was tardy. Thinking like a minister and a lawman and a saddle tramp all at the same time is a challenge." I dropped the pencil back inside the bag and pushed it aside. "Where'd he tip his hand with you?"

"His foreman was careless about shutting the door to his study. Richard sent for him. I overheard just enough to find out where he was sending him from there."

"Tell me about the foreman."

"Jack Kolander, a rough character who thinks he's a devil with women. I've seen how he watches me when he thinks I'm not looking, but he's too smart to take it any further with the boss's wife. He'll never find a billet that pays as well. Richard could hire a full-time ranch manager for less."

"Did you ever ask him what Kolander does to earn it?"

"I just keep the books. Not asking questions I don't need to know the answers to is the trade I made for his not asking me the same."

"I thought you said there were no secrets between you."

"Plainly there are. I never knew how many until he accused me of betraying him by not telling him who you were."

"I can see why that would make you angry enough to come running here."

"I walked. I have a reputation to maintain. And you know me better than to think I'd throw over everything I have because my

313

pride got stung."

I searched her eyes. I didn't know her at all. "You don't want to see me murdered. I'll take that as a compliment. Does this Kolander have a broad West Texas accent?"

"Who doesn't? When I first came here I had to learn a whole new language. For a long time I thought Bob Wire was one of Richard's hands. When I found out it was a kind of fence I sat down and listed the names of all the people I made a fool of myself with and who didn't bother to set me straight. That turned out to be a good thing. You can waste a lot of time learning who your enemies are."

"Who else is he overpaying?"

"Fielo, but that's a favor to me. It costs more to feed a breed ram than to staff a house with Mexicans, so what he makes doesn't scratch the budget. He's quiet, respectful, and he has only the one vice. Can you say the same?"

I let the wind take that one as well. "The others must be in it for a percentage. I'm betting they tent up at the ranch between raids. What buffalos me is why Captain Jordan and his Rangers couldn't tie any of them to descriptions of the Blue Bandannas when they visited."

"I remember that day. Kolander wasn't

around. Someone cut the north fence and he took some men and followed a trail of slaughtered sheep as far as the Nations."

"How many men?"

"Five or six."

"Six. Freemason made sure the gang was absent when Jordan came to call. If the fence was cut, they cut it. If sheep were slaughtered, they slaughtered them. It was a small enough price to pay to keep them out of the hands of the law. It wasn't the first time he went out on a limb when his men were in trouble. You never know what the hired help might let slip when they think their boss has abandoned them."

"But why would Richard take such a risk? He was robbing himself."

"That's how he wanted it to look, and it's why he staged that robbery last week with me as a witness, to draw suspicion away from him. You said yourself he's almost bankrupt. He put his Blue Bandannas up to stealing his payroll, convinced outside investors to make it up, and had them steal that, too; he paid his handpicked bandits out of the first amount and probably cut them in for a piece of the rest and all of whatever they foraged on the side so it wouldn't look like he was the only victim. He pocketed the lion's share. Do you know the details of the trouble he got into up in Montana Territory?"

She watched me. "Is this another attempt to worm information out of me?"

"That time's past. Blackthorne came clean finally, when I pressed him. A dozen years ago Freemason was clerk of the U.S. District Court in Helena. That was shortly after Blackthorne took the bench and two years before I came to work for him. Your husband embezzled twenty thousand dollars from the operating budget and used it to start a sheep ranch near the Canadian border. He registered the land in the name of his assistant, and when an auditor from Washington turned up the shortfall, the assistant clerk was arrested, tried, and convicted of misappropriation of public funds."

Dr. Littlejohn rapped on the door. "That's long enough, Mrs. Freemason," he called. "The brother needs his rest."

She looked at me. We shook our heads simultaneously. She got up, recovered his instrument case, and went to the door. A moment of spirited conversation followed, ending when she passed the bag around the edge of the door, closed it, and turned the key in the lock. She returned to her seat.

I said, "I think you just cost me a parishioner."

"Does it matter?"

"Not to me, but I don't think I'll be named a saint of the Unitarian Church." I rubbed my chest. I was giving my bruised lungs a workout. "It fell apart in the end," I went on. "The assistant's wife hired investigators, who reviewed the records of the transaction at the county seat where the ranch was, and established that his signature was forged. It came too late for the assistant; a highwayman serving ten to fifteen years for stealing U.S. securities picked a fight with him in the federal penitentiary in Deer Lodge and let his brains out with a chunk of masonry."

"How much of this can you prove?"

"It's public record."

Her knuckles tightened on the reticule in her lap. "Richard said he was sentenced to seven years. President Grant pardoned him after three months. Five of the twenty thousand went to the congressman who delivered the Republican vote in seventy-two. All this time I thought Blackthorne's complaint was political."

"The assistant clerk's name was Velasquez. His father was a prisoner of war during the fighting in Mexico; Blackthorne liked him, but Velasquez turned down his offer to sponsor him after the war. When his son came of age, he called in the marker. The Judge is vain and petty, but he believes in justice, the Presbyterian Church, and his personal obligations, in that order. He didn't say it — that damn code he uses takes too long on both ends, and he never explains himself anyway — but my guess is when he heard Freemason's name in connection with the robberies here, he wasn't sure enough of his suspicions to tell me and possibly send me off in the wrong direction. If his hunch was right, I'd stumble on it myself. In a way it was a vote of confidence from the son of a bitch."

"The son of a bitch," she agreed. "I might have gone on thinking I'd pulled myself out of the muck finally."

"Not you. You're too smart for Freemason. You'd have seen through him soon enough."

"Not as soon as you."

"I'm not married to him."

"You're smart enough to outsmart your-self," she said. "You knew when you told him Luther Cherry had confessed to being a spy for the Blue Bandannas he knew you were lying. If Cherry didn't set up that rob-bery on the road to clear himself, it had to have been Richard. You might as well have accused him straight out."

"If I did, he'd have thought I had enough

information to arrest him. As long as he
believed I was still building a case, he had a
chance to prevent me from delivering it.
That's why I turned Captain Jordan away
when he said he wanted to ask Brother Bernard more questions in private. As long as
Freemason thought I was the only one who
suspected him, I could flush him out by
drawing his fire. I did outsmart myself," I
said, nodding. "I didn't think he'd mount a
direct assault on me in the church, his
church. He's more desperate than I
thought."

She shook her head. "Less. He's beaten
the system twice with pardons. Once you're
out of the way he's convinced he's invin-
cible."

"A common failing in men of influence.
You ought to set your sights on a lowly road
agent."

"Page, that's unkind even for you."

I looked at her, and the expression on her
face surprised me more than the bullet
through the window. Moisture glittered like
bits of quartz in the corners of her eyes. If
she'd brought that to a poker table I'd have
cleaned her out.

A floorboard shifted outside the door; the
squeak was sharp in the quiet of the room.
She stood, rustling her skirts and muttering

something about the damn doctor. Before she got to it, the door sprang open and struck the wall on our side. The man who'd kicked it lunged through the opening on the force of his own momentum, grabbed Colleen's shoulder, and spun her to face me with a forearm across her throat. He spun the Spencer rifle in his other hand by the lever, working a round into the chamber, and leveled it at me.

"Beg pardon, Reverend," he said, "it being the Lord's Own Day and all." His speech was as wide as West Texas, muffled a little by the blue bandanna that covered his face to the eyes.

TWENTY-SEVEN

My hand twitched in the direction of the revolver on the nightstand, but I let it fall when he flexed his arm, drawing a strangled croak from Colleen.

"You're square with Jesus, Reverend, but maybe the lady ain't. Push that English pistol off the edge easy."

I did, using the tips of my fingers. The Deane-Adams struck the floor with a thud. The man with the rifle relaxed his grip a notch. Colleen sucked in air in a long draught.

"I'll have that strongbox from the morning," he said. "I heard you raked it in."

"Is that why you shot at me?"

"That was careless. By the time I got to the door the place was crawling. There's still a crowd got their snouts stuck to the windows. I figure if they see you lug that box out they won't think anything about it."

"They will if I'm with a masked man with a rifle."

"You won't be. The lady and me'll just make ourselves to home here till you get back."

"What if I just keep walking?"

"Well, now, that wouldn't set just right with the Almighty. When you get through them pearly gates she'll be waiting with a slug in her head. Same thing if you come back with anybody or anything but that box."

"Is it all right if I get dressed?"

"Sure. We can't have the parson slanching about half naked. Wouldn't be decent."

I slid out from under the sheet on the side opposite where I'd dropped the revolver, retrieved my shirt, collar, and coat from the heap where the doctor had left them when he examined me, and drew them on slowly, my fingers fumbling with the collar button behind my neck. I knew the man and his weapon from the road to Freemason's ranch, and I didn't believe for a second that he'd come just for the church collection. He was Freemason's man; I wasn't to survive the transaction to bear witnesses against his employer. The box was extra incentive, and cover for my murder.

"Jack, I can make up the difference if

you'll just leave. I —"

Jack Kolander, Richard Freemason's foreman, choked her off with his arm. In that instant I saw confusion in his eyes and satisfaction in Colleen's. If the plan was to leave her alive to back up the robbery theory, she'd just tipped it on its head. Plainly, he hadn't orders in case she identified him. The rancher had stopped short of condemning his wife.

I pressed in. "You weren't told some other things. The name's Murdock, not Sebastian. I'm a deputy U.S. marshal."

The confusion crystallized into something else. He'd made up his mind in favor of his own survival, and to hell with Freemason. "That makes things easier. I'd sooner slaughter a wolf than a lamb. Now fetch that box."

I pulled up my braces and turned toward the door, sliding one hand into a sleeve of my rusty black coat.

"I got men on roofs with repeaters," Kolander said, "in case she ain't reason enough to come back. When I hear shooting, I'll put one in her and clear out."

I turned back his way, still half in and half out of the coat. It put me a step closer. "You'll do it anyway, and you'll put one in me too as soon as I show up with the money. Why should I waste the time walking all the way to the church and back?"

"On account of every minute's one more you got, both of you." For emphasis he arched his back, tightening his grip and pulling Colleen off her feet.

That was a mistake.

She'd been preoccupied with keeping both feet on the floor to avoid strangling under her own weight. Now she scissored one leg and raked the heel of her pump down his right shin blade, probably drawing blood. He cursed in a high shrill voice. I whirled my coat underhand in a circle, caught the Spencer's muzzle with the hem, and jerked it toward the ceiling, which blew apart with a shower of plaster chunks and dust when the trigger jerked his finger. In the shock of the moment he relaxed his forearm. Colleen ducked out from under, grasping at the barrel of the rifle with both hands. She failed to gain a purchase, and as he swept it out of her reach he slammed the stock against the side of her head.

She collapsed — on top of me. I'd dived for the Deane-Adams on the floor, but got one foot tangled on the rung of the straight-back chair beside the bed, and all three of us — me, Colleen, and the chair — wound up in a snarl of flesh and bone and pine. I groped for the revolver and found only plank floor.

Something clacked twice, the lever of a repeater jacking a shell into the barrel. A huge black bat flew across my vision; my coat, caught on the front sight of Kolander's Spencer. I wouldn't even see where the bullet was coming from.

A shot cracked; I flinched as if I were hit. Something heavy struck the floor hard enough to shake more plaster from the shattered ceiling. It spilled like salt onto the back of Jack Kolander's white duster, spread like angel's wings where he lay splayed out on his face, his arms flung out in the shape of a cross.

A needle of brimstone stung my nostrils, coming from the barrel of the small slim American Arms pistol in Colleen's kid leather palm. Her reticule lay open on the floor where it had fallen when I'd knocked over the chair.

Gunfire crackled outside. Hollow in the open and bent by the wind, it might have been a string of firecrackers going off; in the West every holiday is an occasion for fireworks. I found the Deane-Adams finally — it had skidded under the bed in the scramble — and got up. Colleen, athletic as ever, was already on her feet. I felt as if a dray had run over my chest, leaving deep ruts. I still feel it sometimes when I've lived wrong.

I nearly shot Captain Jordan coming in the door. Colleen came closer; I caught her elbow with an uphand sweep just as she emptied her second barrel. The little slug dashed yellow splinters out of the door frame just above the Ranger's head. He had on the same clothes I'd seen him in last, riding gear, and carried a sawed-off Stevens ten-gauge shotgun in both hands crossways to his body, like a quarterstaff. His face was red beneath the deep bronze.

His eyes went straight from the distraction of the shot to the body on the floor.

"Dead," I said. "What about the rest?"

"One dead, one on his way. We winged another. One threw up his hands. Two more run off, but we know where they're headed. We followed 'em here from the ranch. I didn't exactly go back to Wichita Falls after I left here the other night," he said.

"I wish I'd known."

"I couldn't get word to you without scaring 'em back into cover." Belatedly, he took off his hat, watching Colleen. "We need to talk to your husband, Mrs. Freemason. You, too, maybe."

"She's out in the open," I said. "She's the one who shot Kolander."

He cradled the shotgun along a forearm, slid the hat off the back of the dead man's head, pulled it up by a fistful of hair, and tore loose the bandanna. It was a stubbled face with sandy moustaches and spider-traces of blood coming from the corners of his mouth. "Kolander, that's the name?" Jordan spoke to Colleen over his shoulder.

"That's him. Richard's at the house, or was when I left. I don't think he'll resist. It's past the time for gunplay. Now it's the lawyers' turn."

"We'll bring our guns along just the same."

I said, "You can't sneak up on him. His house overlooks the whole town."

"He built it to withstand cattle wars," Colleen said. "You can shoot at it all day and all night. All you'll do is break china."

Jordan chewed the ends of his handlebars. In his weathered face I saw faint traces of the fresh features of the young Ranger in the photograph in his office. It had been taken at Fort Sill, where the Comanche Nation had surrendered after breaking its back assaulting a handful of buffalo hunters holed up at Adobe Walls.

"Man has to eat," he said finally. "We'll

wait him out."

Colleen said, "I'll talk to him. I've always been able to make him listen to reason."

"No, ma'am. I'll not put a chip in his hands."

"I don't have to ask your permission. It's my house. You can place me under restraint, but I'll put up a fight. It will take three men. How many do you need to lay siege to a fortress?"

He looked at me. I shook my head. "I wouldn't argue with her. I still have scars."

She said, "He's no ordinary fugitive. He has resources. The chances are he's already put them to work. Why risk panicking him with an attack party?"

"Well, hell," he said; and that was the end of the resistance.

I unhooked my coat from the end of Kolander's Spencer and shrugged into it. The hole he'd blown through it had smoldered for a while, but it had stopped, leaving an evil smell. "You fixing to come with us?" Jordan asked.

"If you'll have me. This is the first time I've had the blinders off since Helena."

"Let's get to it, then, before our past life catches up with us."

I asked him for a moment and went to get my Bible. Colleen and Jordan watched in silence as I read over the dead man. When I finished I closed the book, put it in my side pocket, and took off the clerical collar. I put it on the bed and picked up the Deane-Adams.

TWENTY-EIGHT

Afternoon was well along; moving into position, our party threw saguaro-shaped shadows halfway across the street. The sun painted crimson stripes on the wrought-iron spikes that crowned the American castle on its man-made hill and reflected in flat sheets off the mullioned windows facing west, turning them into armor plate. There was nothing preposterous about the place now; it might have stood through the Crusades and expected to stand until the end of all things.

The businesses on both sides of the street were closed for the holy day, but Jordan had sent a man — it was Corporal Thomson, the young Ranger who'd put me up overnight in Wichita Falls, with a wife expecting a child — to roust out the shopkeepers stacking stock and recording inventory and persuade the residents of the houses to stay inside and away from the windows. It had taken him half an hour, but the captain hadn't wanted to alert Freemason by sending a party. He was being overcautious; all our quarry had to do was look out and see all the merchants locking up at the same time to know something was in the wind. In times past — Texas being Texas — the neighbors would have been recruited to serve in the assault, supplying their own weapons and ammunition, but the second generation of pioneers had moved into the protected category, like the people they'd left behind in the cities of the East. In twenty years, maybe less, citizens' posses would be a part of history, and professionals firmly in place to defend the peace unassisted. There would be a policeman on every corner, and no more deputy marshals required to ride circuit over an area the size of New Hampshire. It was progressive, inevitable, but I smelled in it the stink of my own grave.

As the light shifted, so did the demeanor of the gaunt house on its unnatural heap. It looked vulnerable — indecently so, as if by design. The heavy siege shutters I'd noticed on my first visit yawned wide, as if Freemason had declared open house. The thought chilled me there in the bright sun, in the hot wind. I felt suddenly as if we were the ones being hunted.

Jordan, directing operations from the deep doorway of the Catholic church, saw what I saw and reached a different conclusion. "Lit out, I expect. If he's forted up at the ranch, I'm going to have to send to San Antonio for more men. It'll take days."

I said nothing. When the Rangers were all in place, stationed at second-story windows and in narrow alleys, Colleen Bower emerged from the First Unitarian church. She'd put herself back together after the wrestling match in the parsonage, pinned her hat in place, and with her reticule wound around her wrist (without the pistol, which Jordan had taken charge of), the first lady of Owen might have been returning home from one of her regular errands. When she drew abreast of us, I stepped forward. The captain touched my arm.

"There's nothing for it if she gets hurt," he said. "The governor don't pay enough pension to look after my crippled cousin."

"It's the best way to take him alive. If he turns himself in through her, he'll go to his lawyers instead of his gunmen. Anyway, you've seen what happens when someone tries to hold her down."

I caught up with her and we walked like two strangers bound in the same direction, without speaking.

We climbed the long flight of steps to the front door. She'd asked for five minutes alone with her husband; I'd determined to give her two. I hung back while she twisted the bell, waited, then twisted it again. It rang away back in a place of desertion.

She turned my way. "Fielo only leaves the house when Richard sends him. He can't think it's an ordinary day."

I didn't know whether she meant Freemason or the servant, but I wasn't sure of that either way. Those spread shutters haunted me. I didn't agree with Jordan that he'd flown to cover at the ranch. The situation was just the one the house had been planned and built for. I'd faced apparent traps before, but now I felt as if I were fighting the urge to walk right into one. The oath I'd taken had said nothing about battling my own nature.

I settled the point. When she untied her bag and fished out a key, I took it from her and moved her aside with a firm hand on her elbow. I drew the Deane-Adams and unlocked the door.

No one shot at me when I eased it open, using the thick door for a shield. The foyer was empty except of furniture. So were the adjoining rooms when I prowled through them, the baronial dining hall and a long kitchen with an enormous white-enamel Jewel stove and, suspended from the ceiling, clusters of copper and cast-iron pots and skillets. The air smelled of stale grease and dry herbs, as if no meal had been prepared there in months.

A tiny room off the kitchen contained a cot, a small chest of drawers, and a wash basin on a stand; the servant's quarters, abandoned also. A back door opened on a path worn through grass to a privy out back. I didn't check that. It was no place to hide with a fortress waiting.

There was one door I hadn't tried, but I didn't think it was for me to try it. I returned to the front step where Colleen, obedient for once, waited. She asked me if I'd looked in the study.

"No."

She read my face. I wished I knew what she saw there. I was behind it and I had no idea.

She said, "He feels safe there."

I nodded and stepped aside. She looked at me, not so much curious as inviting an explanation. "It's your house."

She came in and I followed her down the hallway, three steps behind with the revolver pointed toward the ceiling.

She knocked at the stout paneled door, spoke his name. No one answered. She tried the knob. "Locked. He has the only key."

She stepped away without being asked while I hammered on the door. My fist boomed like cannon practice; no strategic satisfaction. It was the quietest house I'd ever been in. Even a fallen-in shack on the prairie has something scuttling around inside.

I didn't try kicking. It was too much door and it had a heavy brass lock.

One of the sculptures that decorated the house was a bronze casting of a Knight Templar drawing his sword, the inescapable Masonic symbol emblazoned on his shield. It stood three feet high at the end of the hallway on a tall fluted pedestal with a marble base. I pocketed the Deane-Adams, hoisted the statue off its stand, and signaled Colleen to stand clear. I set myself and rammed the lock. It held, but on the second try I put a dent in the knight's helmet and got a splitting sound. A long shard of polished wood came away from the frame on the third. I laid the statue on the floor, fisted the revolver, and threw a heel at the lock. The door flew open with less resistance than expected and I caught the frame hard with my right shoulder to avoid falling

335

headlong. It was the pulpit all over again; pain racked me from front to back, but the muzzle of the .45 found Richard Freemason in his embossed-leather chair as if I'd trained it.

He sat slumped in his shirtsleeves and a scarlet waistcoat, turned a quarter of the way on his swivel toward the tall massive desk. He hadn't moved even when the door exploded against the wall.

I saw why when I approached him and turned the chair my way by its back. He wasn't wearing a red waistcoat, or one of any other color. The knife that had nearly separated his head from his trunk had opened his jugular all down the front of his shirt. Only the whites of his eyes showed, and they were no more pale than his face.

I heard a high keening sound, but Colleen wasn't crying. It was my own breath straining to get in and out after another blow to the lungs and the strain of using a hunk of bronze the size of a newborn calf for a battering ram. I found out later the thing weighed a hundred and forty pounds. It took two men to put it back on its pedestal.

No, she wasn't crying, but her voice was tight. "He's taken his own life."

I didn't mention that there was no knife. For all I was aware, she knew where it was.

■ ■ ■ ■

She didn't. The Rangers found him finally, in the little privy I hadn't bothered to look inside. In my defense I'll add that they only thought of it after they'd searched the house from the upstairs bedrooms, the ballroom with its fabulous chandelier, and water closet to the coal furnace in the basement.

He was propped primly with his back against the plank wall, sitting in his white linen uniform on the flipped-down seat, his long brown hands dangling between his thighs, the wrists sliced open almost neatly with what was probably the same knife he'd used to cut Freemason's throat, a butcher's tool with a curved blade still razor sharp after it had done its work; part of a set from the kitchen, it lay on the floor between his sandaled feet. A bottle of Hermitage with a teaspoonful of whiskey left in the bottom stood beside him on the seat. The liquor had thinned his blood, accelerating the process, but he was an old man and his heart had given out first. Colleen cried when she was told, as she hadn't for her husband. Her affection for the gentle old manservant was genuine.

I guessed what it was about, with intuition

337

pumped up like my strength under pressure and pain, but I kept it to myself. It all came out when they searched him and found the note, in the same pocket where he'd placed the key he'd used to lock his master's body in the study. He'd wanted time to write it and see the thing through. He'd used a sheet of Colleen's notepaper, as if he refused to touch Freemason's Masonic stationery. It was written in a surprisingly fine hand, in Spanish; but the translation could wait. He'd signed it "Fielo Velasquez."

THE THIRTEENTH APOSTLE

I have glorified thee on the earth: I have finished the work which thou gavest me to do.

— JOHN 17:4

Beyond some follow-up questions to my report, Judge Blackthorne and I never discussed my time in Texas again. He went to his grave without another word on the subject. I can't make the same claim, although mine lies open before me. I made mistakes that cost lives, souls too, and while I'm less certain than ever about what's waiting, Owen is one burden I'm determined to leave behind.

I have to include Eldred Griffin among the casualties. The doll's house in the Catholic cemetery was shut up when I went there to return the shabby sheaf of sermons, the shutters fastened and a padlock on the front door. His death, punctuation to the gossip that had hounded him for years, was still lively after two weeks: His wife, Esther, had gone to his study to pour him a second cup of tea and found him dead on the floor, fallen in a heap from his chair, where he'd been seated at his writing table sipping his first and reading an Aramaic text from the third century. Grubs hindered the growth of sod between the graves, arsenite of lead was discovered in quantity on the premises, and one or two details about the condition of the corpse persuaded a coroner's jury to rule death by misadventure. No suspicion fell upon Esther. The rumor of suicide moved Father Medavoy of the Cathedral of the Sacred Hearts of Jesus and Mary to refuse interment in hallowed ground. Esther boxed up the remains and shipped them to her sister in Michigan, accompanying them in a day coach. I never found out if she sought or found reunion with her other relations. I wonder frequently if Griffin's part in my impostiture had deprived him of his last shred of faith, or if he kept it and like Judas in his Easter sermon chose eternal damnation to punish himself for questioning. Either way his fate lies heavily upon me.

Dr. Lawrence Lazarus Little, proprietor of the Traveling Tabernacle, settled in California, and forty years later at the age of eighty-two became one of the first ministers to preach over the ether. On certain nights when the air was clear, his five hundred-watt "Electric Pulpit" came crackling over my set in Los Angeles. The booming voice had grown reedy with time, and I realized then that that astonishing baritone had provided ninety percent of his message, taking the place of conviction. Griffin had seen past it at its peak.

Richard Freemason's eight-hundred-acre sheep ranch was broken up by his widow and sold to satisfy his creditors, including the State of Texas, to which he owed property taxes in the thousands. The largest parcel went to the brother of a bishop in Dublin, who took pleasure in stripping away all the Masonic symbols, including the brand.

I never heard what became of Captain Andrew Jackson Jordan of the Texas Rangers. I assume he retired, because Governor Ireland transferred the rest of the Wichita Falls office to San Antonio shortly after the last of the Blue Bandannas was captured and sentenced to hang, and Jordan had made no secret of his opposition to committing all the Rangers' best men to the bandit problem on the border at the expense of the panhandle. I picture him living out the rest of his days smoking his pipe on the front porch on some small spread where he looked after his cousin.

Its abandonment by the Rangers, together with the bad reputation left by Freemason, took Owen out of the running for a railroad spur from Wichita Falls. It passed south to create Amarillo, which promptly became the principal city in a region the size of many states. That should have been the end of Owen, but it had demonstrated its tenacity before. The sheep trade, with a shot in the arm from the newly passed fence-cutting law, kept the town alive, at the cost of the saloon business; for some reason sheep hands in those days were more conservative carousers than cowboys. Freemason's house, I'm told, still stands — converted, appropriately, into a county home for the insane.

I'm living out my time in a comfortable bungalow with a view of a swimming pool, the latest in a series of enthusiasms to claim Southern California. I don't swim — one immersion is enough for one lifetime, even if it's a better prospect than a buffalo wallow — but the improbably blue water is pleasant to look at, a rare luxury for a "movie," which is a noxious class restricted by many landlords. Movies are employees of the picture business. I make my rent peddling my experience to producers, who admire to include an old frontier lawman in press releases promoting their westerns. I'm freelancing now. I had a nice billet with United Artists, Chaplin and Pickford's outfit, but they let me go when a newspaper hack in the pay of a rival studio wrote that Page Murdock had been gunned down in Helena in 1884, and that I was an impostor. It wasn't the first time Blackthorne's harebrained ruse cast doubt on my identity; but the place is rotten with frauds, and I manage to avoid eviction by the grace of UA's less discriminating competitors. How long it will last I can't say. I'll be clay soon enough, so I have no worries about corporeal matters. My spiritual condition is something else.

I'm writing down my confessions. They'd fill a good-size trunk, and I have to sit on the old Wells, Fargo strongbox I keep them in to lock it. It's bolted to the floor to discourage theft. It's a small town, word gets around, and scenarists are always pestering me for a look, which means they want to loot them for ideas. A safe deposit box would be more convenient — at least I wouldn't have to guard the pages at night with the venerable Deane-Adams — but I chased too many bandits in the old days to place much faith in banks. Anyway, I'm writing not to be read, but for the sake of my immortal soul. I search the Bible for comfort, with its pages falling out of the worn-out binding, and I say my prayers every night, mostly for the dead and partly for myself, because I sent more than a few of them to hell and maybe one or two to heaven. My soul isn't pure.

Fielo Velasquez left a stain. I didn't put that knife in his hand, but I might have prevented him from taking it up. He was the right age, the right nationality, and I should have seen something in the mysterious way he came to work for Richard Freemason, especially after I read that coded message about the son of Blackthorne's old friend who had died a death in prison that should have been Freemason's. I don't know why Fielo waited so long, or why he chose that day of all days to take a father's revenge, except perhaps that he might have sensed that time was running short and that he was about to be cheated out of it. Old men are prescient, I know now. And like Griffin he'd followed the example set by Judas.

I suppose that puts Freemason's fate on

my head as well, but I don't spend as much time praying for him as I do most of the others.

Colleen buried the old man in the cemetery maintained by the First Unitarian church. I don't know who presided, because I'd left by then. Fielo was barred, of course, from the Catholic, but a number of mourners came out for the service in support of the first widow of Owen, whose bereavement under the circumstances seemed to have removed her at least temporarily from that order of women that is accepted because of position but not respected. She had a carriage packed with luggage and left town directly from the graveside. Her late husband's legal firm in St. Louis sent someone out to supervise the disposition of the ranch and the house in town.

Luther Cherry's widow experienced the same social promotion, but of a more permanent nature. After a respectable year she married a Missouri state senator who went on to serve two terms in Congress and may be our next vice president, or a member of a railroad board of directors, which is the logical alternative. She may have been worth the preposterous expense of writing her by special delivery from Texas, at that. I feel no guilt for what happened to Cherry, but I ask forgiveness for maligning him afterward, necessary as it was to flush Freemason from cover.

These days I spend a lot of time thinking about Colleen Bower. We met a few times after Owen, but I lost her trail after Blackthorne died and Washington sliced his jurisdiction into several easily corruptible pieces. Some years ago I thought I recognized a familiar figure in a *Saturday Evening Post* piece about an old *gringa,* name unknown, who organized arms shipments to Pancho Villa from El Paso and delivered provisions to revolutionists hiding in the caves of Chihuahua from General Pershing's punitive expedition following the raid on Columbus, New Mexico. The artist's rendition taken from an American poster offering a reward for her capture resembled Colleen around the eyes, but her hair had gone gray and the desert sun had cracked her fair complexion, so I wasn't sure. Villa's men called her *Nuestra Madre de la Orilla:* Our Lady of the Border. U.S. authorities called her an enemy of the state. That sums her up in my opinion.

AUTHOR'S NOTE:
THE WORD OUT WEST

The motif of the gun-toting preacher is nothing new in the literature and cinema of the American frontier. Oxymoronic though he may seem, the figure of the white-collared man in black with Scripture in hand and a revolver on his hip recurs frequently in the tapestry of the New World's answer to the mythos of Greece and Rome, and he has a historical foundation. The author is pleased to provide an incomplete checklist of those works that have celebrated him:

Barton, Barbara. *Pistol Packin' Preachers: Circuit Riders of Texas.* Lanham, Maryland: A Republic of Texas Press Book, Taylor Trade Publishing, 2005.
Barton's account, with a foreword by the great Western novelist Elmer Kelton, provides an eminently readable history of

itinerant preaching in our most western state, with anecdotes both harrowing and rollicking about the struggle to bring Christianity to the wilderness. An entertaining piece of cocktail-party conversation appears wherever the book falls open.

Phares, Ross. *Bible in Pocket, Gun in Hand: The Story of Frontier Religion.* Lincoln, Nebraska: Bison Books, The University of Nebraska Press, 1971.

First published in 1964, Phares' volume roams over the broader territory of the frontier, with a strong emphasis on the raw humor of ecclesiastical doings on the border of civilization. This is a book to pick up and read at random whenever the reader needs a lift.

Five Card Stud. Directed by Henry Hathaway, starring Dean Martin, Robert Mitchum, Inger Stevens, Roddy McDowall, and Katherine Justice. 1968.

A good old oater of a Western movie, this old-fashioned whodunit set against a backdrop of desert and plain pits gambler Martin, in vintage Rat Pack persona, against Mitchum's quick-on-the-draw minister with a private agenda. Critic Leonard Maltin calls it "probably Hathaway's worst Western," but that hollowed-out Bible with a pocket pistol concealed inside is worth the price of the rental. Shallow, but enormously entertaining.

The Gun and the Pulpit. Starring Marjoe Gortner.

Production details on this 1970s made-for-TV movie are nearly nonexistent, but Gortner, famous for a short time as a child evangelist, made an impression in an even shorter acting career as a gunfighter posing as a preacher. The film resurfaces occasionally under the title *The Gun and the Bible,* a simplistic choice possibly predicated on the belief that most viewers don't know what a pulpit is.

Heaven with a Gun. Directed by Lee H. Katzin, starring Glenn Ford, Carolyn Jones, Barbara Hershey, John Anderson, and David Carradine. 1969.

Ford, who was never anything less than stalwart, puts in a solid performance in the *Shane*-like role of a former man of violence compelled by circumstances to strap on a gunbelt under his frock coat. One of those stirring movies in which a cowed community is shamed by its spiritual advisor into taking its fate in its own hands. (John Carradine, David's father, deserves honorable mention for playing clergy so often — most memorably as the tragic Jim Casy in *The Grapes of Wrath* — as to qualify for common-law ordination.)

Pale Rider. Directed by Clint Eastwood, starring Clint Eastwood, Michael Moriarty, Carrie Snodgress, Christopher Penn, and John Russell. 1985.

Eastwood's spooky savior wears a clerical collar and answers to "Preacher," but he spouts more bullets than gospel in a nearly scene-for-scene plagiarism of *Shane,* with a heavy overlay of his earlier *High Plains Drifter.* Former *Lawman* star Russell is hypnotic in his last role, but it's a dreary film and misses all the subtlety of its inspiration.

ABOUT THE AUTHOR

Loren D. Estleman is the winner of multiple awards for his Western writing, including five Spurs, two Stirrups, and three Western Heritage Awards. He lives in Whitmore Lake, Michigan.